J.S. Lame

Maryland Slavery and Maryland Chivalry

SALZWASSER
VERLAG

J.S. Lame

Maryland Slavery and Maryland Chivalry

Reprint of the original, first published in 1858.

1st Edition 2023 | ISBN: 978-3-37515-182-9

Verlag (Publisher): Salzwasser Verlag GmbH, Zeilweg 44, 60439 Frankfurt, Deutschland
Vertretungsberechtigt (Authorized to represent): E. Roepke, Zeilweg 44, 60439 Frankfurt, Deutschland
Druck (Print): Books on Demand GmbH, In de Tarpen 42, 22848 Norderstedt, Deutschland

MARYLAND SLAVERY

AND

MARYLAND CHIVALRY.

CONTAINING THE

LETTERS OF "JUNIUS," ORIGINALLY PUBLISHED
IN ZION'S HERALD:

TOGETHER WITH A

BRIEF HISTORY OF THE CIRCUMSTANCES THAT PROMPTED
THE PUBLICATION OF THOSE LETTERS.

ALSO A

SHORT ACCOUNT OF THE PERSECUTION SUFFERED BY THE AUTHOR
AT THE HANDS OF SOUTHERN SLAVEHOLDERS.

BY

Rev. J. S. LAME,

OF THE PHILADELPHIA ANNUAL CONFERENCE.

PHILADELPHIA:
COLLINS, PRINTER, 705 LODGE ALLEY.
1858.

PREFACE.

SINCE our violent expulsion from the field of labor to which we were duly appointed, we have been frequently solicited to publish a brief and impartial history of the origin of the letters of "Junius;" together with an account of the proceedings of our Southern friends when they became apprised of our complicity with those letters.

That the following pages are free from error, is more than we can hope. That they are exempt from intentional mistake we are fully assured.

If we have incautiously soiled the fair fame of the humblest, we will be most happy to apologize for, and as far as possible repair, the injury.

If we have misstated facts—if we have arrived at wrong conclusions—if, on the perplexing subject of slavery, we are "zealously affected, but not well," we are open to conviction.

We do most devoutly abominate oppression in all its forms and phases. The great deep of our soul has been stirred by the sights we have seen and the sounds we have heard; and we are deeply desirous of contributing the widow's mite to the treasury of human freedom.

May God defend the right!

J. S. LAME.

VILLAGE GREEN, *September*, 1858.

MARYLAND SLAVERY AND MARYLAND CHIVALRY.

As it is known to the Church that the author of the following pages has been recently expelled from the field of labor to which he was appointed at the late session of the Philadelphia Annual Conference, it is but just that the church should be acquainted with the crime with which he is charged—for which he has been tried and adjudged guilty—and is now suffering the penalty of expatriation.

In order to have a proper understanding of the letters published in *Zion's Herald* (Boston), and republished in this pamphlet, it will be necessary to present some preliminary facts and observations.

We were born and educated in the State of Pennsylvania. Being incessantly pursued by a voice that importunately cried, "Wo unto you if you preach not the Gospel"—and believing that our only road to heaven lay through the Pulpit, we reluctantly consented to enter the ministerial ranks. In our twentieth year we became a member of the Philadelphia Conference. In the spring of 1856, we were appointed to labor in Slaveholding territory. Up to that period, we had never read an elaborate treatise on the subject of slavery. Having frequently read conflicting newspaper accounts, we had arrived at the conclusion to ignore the whole subject, and turn it over to the tender mercies of the politicians. The question of the right of property in man had never been settled, for it had never been investigated; and our presumption was that the condition of the bond was superior to the condition of the colored free. Thus we were prepared to apologize for, if not defend the institution.

A few months after our arrival on the circuit, being in a country store, a man of wealth and distinction commenced talking to one of his slaves who was present, accusing him of keeping swine that he fed from his master's cornfield. Growing furious as he spoke, he avowed his determination to send South for a nigger-driver, and designed to put a whip in one hand, and a pistol in the other, and drive his slaves into measures, and if they resisted to shoot them down like dogs. The poor slave, though a man of years, appeared like the quivering aspen, scarce venturing a word of reply. We trembled as we thought of the tremendous power of the master over his defenceless slave.

Occupying the kitchen attached to the house in which we resided, were five negroes. They were utterly destitute of a bed. A few filthy rags constituted their only couch. During the excessively severe winter of 1856, as we lay on our own comfortable bed, our heart ached as we thought of the destitution and suffering of those poor slaves, who had so few friends to sympathize with them, no kind hand to minister to their necessities, no mother's gentle care in directing their erring· steps, and with minds utterly untutored. In the depths of winter, through the long cold nights, while their master and mistress were reposing on comfortable beds—the product of those negroes' labor—they lay, with the wind whistling through the quarter, while the snow became their covering. Thoughts suggested by these circumstances kept wakeful our midnight hours. One of those slaves, a boy of 16, in bondage for a number of years, seizes a favorable opportunity to go and see his father, without his master's consent; and for this atrocious crime, his term of bondage was doubled.

These facts presenting themselves to our mind, forced us to reflect, and to make an investigation of the *theory* of slavery.

The more we read—the more we reflected on the abstract question —and the more minutely we watched the practical operations and developments of the system, the more fully we became settled in the conclusion that such a system is utterly repugnant to the teachings of the Bible. And such were the abominations of the traffic, as practised by church members and ministers, by professors and pub-.licans, that we were driven to the admission that, considering the circumstances, the American is the worst system of slavery that ever saw the sun ; and, with our eye fixed on the fires of the last judgment, we aver that such shocking abomination, grinding oppression, cruel barbarities, unrelenting despotism, and foul impurities, are practised on the Eastern Shore of Maryland, as would have disgraced Earth's most barbarous age and nation.

And yet the system with which these atrocities seem inseparably connected, finds apologists innumerable in the church, and even among God's ministers.

We consoled ourselves with the thought that the Discipline of the M. E. Church, both in letter and spirit, was opposed to slavery. Turning to page 21, we found what we, in our simplicity, thought was a prohibitory law on the subject of buying and selling slaves; but we were soon informed, by commentators on the Discipline, that this law prohibited traffic in the foreign slave trade. That is, a rule of the M. E. Church forbids its members to become pirates. What a stupendous pitch of morality that law supposes !

The Discipline certainly declares slaveholders ineligible to official station in the church; but the members of the Board of Stewards owned at least 30 slaves, and bought, bred, beat, and sold them *ad libitum*. One member of that board we had frequently heard make the boastful assertion, that the moment his servants were dissatisfied and wished another master, they were at perfect liberty to go. So, taking the good brother at his own proposal, one night the whole *posse* took French leave ; but no sooner was the fact known that they had gone—than a large reward was offered for their apprehension and recovery.

Thus we have indicated the position we occupied up to the spring of 1857, firmly established in the belief of the great wickedness of slavery, but not settled as to the proper means for its removal. Ministers of age and wisdom deprecated all agitation of the subject, discountenancing its introduction into the pulpit and the press.

In the month of April, 1857, we received our appointment to Snow Hill Circuit, Worcester Co., Md., the circuit extending almost to the line of Virginia. We entered upon our labor with the determination to earnestly and honorably endeavor to discharge all the duties of our position. Here we were more fully impressed with the evils of slavery: portraits of its shocking abominations hang as distinct and prominent pictures on the walls of memory. Here we were able to learn how the slaves present so fine an appearance on the Sabbath, and on holiday occasions. After they have spent the day in laboring for their masters, a portion of the night is usually employed in making baskets, brooms, &c.; and no sooner did a load of wood arrive at the parsonage than a number were on the ground to secure the task of cutting and splitting, after nightfall.

I have held frequent conversations with the poor sufferers, as they toiled at the wood. I asked one poor fellow, the property of a drunken master: "Are you free ?" "Ah ! no, massa !" " They say that Maryland is to be a free State." "Ah! I'se heard dat too often, massa!"

One old, back-bent, hard-handed man of toil stated that, in his younger days, he labored all day for his master, and spent the whole of six consecutive nights working for his personal benefit; and that, when he expressed his wish to marry a free girl, his master, to intimidate him, threatened to sell him South. He married a slave, and, as a consequence, that wife, with a portion of his children, are now probably in the rice swamps of the South. But he got another wife and children. Ought we to have expelled him for the crime of adultery? We pause for a reply. As the result of excessive labor, and great exposure, his spine is curved, his limbs twisted and distorted, and he stands as an animated exhibition of the beauties of bondage, and as a mute appeal to indignant Heaven for retributive justice.

Another affecting instance of the helplessness of the slave we found in his incompetency to hold religious services except in the presence of a legally authorized white man. It sometimes happened that, owing to the apathy of the whites, no protector could be provided. At one of the churches on the circuit, the colored people were compelled to suspend their meetings for many months. The authority ceded to the protector is not transferable. The colored people of an adjoining circuit convened a meeting for the purpose of preaching a funeral sermon. The authorized protector being indisposed, he sent his license to a friend, who repaired to the place of meeting, and the exercises commenced. During their progress, a constable entered, dispersed the assembly, arrested the white man, and carried him before a magistrate. Having frequently preached for our colored members, we have seen most astounding displays of religious excitement. The house may be resounding with loud Hallelujah's, and a score of mourners at the altar, may be importunately imploring mercy; yet, at a certain hour of the night, the proceedings must be stopped, the lights extinguished, and the people driven like swine from the house.

One evening, owing to an extraordinary effusion of divine power, the meeting was delayed a few moments after the fatal hour. As we retired from the house, the patrol, with staff in hand, and posse at his side, was wending his way to the meeting, and, as we were informed, accelerated the speed of some of the tardy worshippers, and then returned to a hotel to spend the night in a noisy frolic.

If holy matrimony, among the higher circles of society, sometimes degenerates into a "matter of money," it certainly finds its counterpart among the enslaved circles; or, it may be more aptly termed, a mere "matter of the master." He can *proscribe and prohibit it* at pleasure.

A slave, belonging to a Methodist of extensive wealth, waited on the writer, and designated an evening on which he wished to be married, and brought with him, as usual in such cases, a certificate from the master which we insert:—

Mr. Lane you may marry my man John to my girl An. i give my consent.
(Signed)   J. S.

We told *plain* John that he ought to ask "*massa* John" for a dollar to give the preacher for getting married; and John brought the munificent sum of twenty-five cents.

A poor fellow came to the parsonage, and complained that he could not see his wife; he had worked for her master, and when he asked for his wages he was refused, and ordered to leave the house. We replied: "Your wife is the property of her master; he can dispose of her as he pleases; and you must submit. We can point to no relief." We have yet to find a colored person that had any confidence in the piety of that man who holds his fellow-beings in bondage.

Having been invited to the house of a free colored man, to marry a colored couple, we found from one to two score of their friends present, both bond and free. Perceiving that they might express themselves plainly with safety, they seized the occasion to express their contempt for the principles and piety of slaveholders. And we discovered that, to avoid disagreeable consequences, the slave may bow and scrape, and say "massa," and be servilely obsequious, while infinite contempt may burn in his bosom. One intelligent-looking fellow said: "Doesn't want to hear Mr. Quigley preach again; he was once preachin in dis hur circuit, when he called to the *niggers* to make less noise." One who was venerable for years and piety, exclaimed: "Honeys, de Massa will hear for dem dat's bound; every day I prays to God for deliverance." What do you think of your local preacher that has recently sold his slave south? "Doesn't want to hear em preach; doesn't want to see him no how; takes no shine to em." But he was prompted by the purest motives to purchase that man; he was bought at his own solicitation. "*Umph!*" accompanied by a shake of the head highly expressive of incredulity.

But a brother told me some of the slaves don't want to be free. "Some *others do*, den." "You are free, are you not, Uncle?" "Yes, bless God! I jumped dis high (about five feet from the ground) when I carried massa de *las* money for my body." "I doesn't bleves dat man il get to heben dat sells his brother." This was followed by a loud and general burst of laughter.

The bride and groom appeared; the knot was tied; after which, we sat down to a well filled table. $1 50 was made up for the preacher. We stepped into our sulky, and was soon in the village.

In conversation, a short time subsequently, with a slaveholder, he gave the following account of the master of one of the negroes present at the wedding party. This master seemed to have been a regular Legree. He acted on the principle of, "Laws, no use fussin with the critters—work em up—kill em off." He almost starved his negroes, and punished them most severely for crimes real and imaginary. On one occasion the narrator was at the house of the master, when some chickens were missing. The theft was attributed to a certain slave. He was called up and denied the charge; but, as the narrator was leaving the farm, he heard the sound of heavy blows, and the voice of the slave crying: "Oh, my God, massa." But no helping hand was nigh to deliver him. The slave who was at the wedding attempted to abscond; he got as far as the lower portion of the State of Delaware, and was apprehended. His master placed one end of a rope around his neck, and fastened the other to his carriage, and thus brought him home in hot haste.

We needed no works of fiction to illustrate the evils of slavery. They were seen in the social, civil, spiritual, and mental degradation of the blacks, and in its corresponding influence on the whites.

The state of our mind may be inferred from the foregoing facts, and from our experience as narrated in "Junius'" letters.

In the epistolary correspondence of the writer with a northern friend, we expressed some strong anti-slavery sentiments; and by that friend the writer was subsequently introduced to Rev. J. D. Long as a brother of kindred views and feelings. It was then he announced his determination of writing a book on slavery; and we encouraged him in the enterprise. During the summer of that year, the publication came to hand. It was read, and re-read—thoughtfully, prayerfully, tearfully, alas, alas! Our heart gave its verdict in its favor. It was shown to a few select friends, and by them pronounced an "accurately executed daguerreotype of slavery, on the Maryland Peninsula; and a pretty faithful mirror of Maryland Methodism. This," it was added, "is just the book the case requires. We have had enough works on the abstract question of slavery. Former authors, in treating of the institution, have spoken in general terms as to locality and character; but this locates the evil right in our midst, on the Eastern Shore of Maryland, in the M. E. Church: and it is unanswerable, though sweeping in its denunciations." We met, a little circle of us, aware that we were sinning against the sentiment of the South; and the book was read amid sighs and tears, and cries of "That's true; that's true."

Judge of our surprise on hearing that Rev. T. J. Quigley, a native of a free State, had preferred charges against the author of "Pictures of Slavery;" and, further, that he had been dubbed D. D. by a Southern literary institution. We were pained; we devoutly believed J. D. Long was right, and T. J. Quigley wrong. Our idea of the tyrannical and inquisitorial character of those charges, finds expression in the following excerpt from an editorial in *Zion's Herald* :—

"As it regards the case of Rev. John D. Long, we do not wish to antici-pate ecclesiastical decisions. If to publish a book of facts and reflections is in that latitude a sin, he must suffer. If the light-hating, mouth-sealing, bookseller-banishing, mail-robbing practices of the South are to enter the sacred precincts of Methodist Episcopal Conferences, and a brother is to be tried, deposed, and ecclesiastically decapitated for publishing a book, every assertion of which is confirmed by a cloud of witnesses, let us know it, and let the world know it. We shall make diligent inquiry, the next day, whether we live in the United States or Naples, whether this is the Methodist Episcopal Church or the Roman Catholic Church, whether it is the Philadel-phia Conference or the Holy Inquisition! And, moreover, we shall all very clearly understand what kind of defence our Conferences in slaveholding territory require when they think themselves misrepresented. They do not furnish counter statements, nor literary champions of the same metal, but they resort to obsolete, mediæval, and pagan weapons. They substitute ecclesiastical for printing machinery, the battering ram for the pen, the cudgel for the syllogism, and excommunication for a manly utterance of belief. So be it. All sorts of fungi grow in the shade, and the rule is a divine one—"By their fruits shall ye know them."

A beloved brother was charged with unchristian conduct. What was our duty in the premises? Remain silent, and allow truth to suffer and the character of a brother to be ruined, without a friendly attempt at defence?

These were most perplexing questions. They were carried to the throne of grace, and wisdom asked of God; and, believing we were divinely directed, we resolved to proceed. But we were in an enemy's county. Our views would be exceedingly obnoxious to the community in which we lived; we had never written for the press; our secret could be intrusted to none; if we published, it was necessary to do so over an assumed name; should the author be discovered, he would suffer proscription and persecution, if not personal violence. But duty was imperative, and we determined to proceed.

The following are the letters as originally published in *Zion's Herald :*—

LETTER I.

December 2, 1857.

MR. EDITOR : Having this morning quite unexpectedly received a copy of your paper, I was much pleased with its contents, particularly with the spirit of liberality that seemed to breathe through its columns. It is an old saying, and true as old, that " experience is the best teacher." Experience has taught and still is teaching me that I am no longer a freeman, and therefore I am able to estimate the value of freedom of speech by the pain of its loss. I happen, Mr. Editor, to have been born, and to have lived in a State that can emphatically affirm—

> " Here freedom spreads her banners wide,
> And casts her soft and hallowed ray ;"

and to have had a mother from whose lips I learned to love liberty and hate oppression. But my early lessons seem to cost me nearly as much as Daniel's cost him at the court of Darius, for my field of ministerial labor lies in that part of our country where public sentiment puts a padlock on the mouth of God's ministers. In other words, I am an humble member of a border conference.

Perhaps I might contribute the widow's mite to the treasury of human freedom by giving a sketch of my experience and observations in this slaveholding district of the M. E. Church. During the earlier years of my ministry, it was my fortune to labor in a portion of territory where slavery was excluded by religion and by law. At length, by no effort of my own, I was appointed to a circuit in the " sunny South." I was rather pleased than otherwise with the change, as I had heard conflicting accounts of our border work. I had seen and heard glowing panegyrics upon Southern hospitality— that preachers were sometimes spoiled by over-indulgence ; and an

opportunity was now offered me to practically prove the truth of
these statements. So, nerving my moral constitution against the
descent of this vast avalanche of Southern generosity, and with a
settled determination to act on the principle of non-intervention
with regard to this darling institution, I at length arrived at my
circuit, and did really find the people kind and hospitable. But, as
I have now filled my sheet, my experience on my circuit must form
the subject of another communication. Till then, adieu.

JUNIUS.

LETTER II.

December 23, 1857.

Mr. Editor: My last communication closed with the announce-
ment of my arrival on my southern circuit. Having heard much
discussion on the subject of slavery, and having heard the conserva-
tives magnify the Christian conduct of the master, and the generally
happy condition of the slaves, I am frank to confess that my mind
was favorably impressed with regard to the institution, and I designed
to apologize for, if not to defend, the system.

Here I made my first entry into that mysterious appendage to all
southern domestic establishments, "the quarter," *alias* a kitchen.
Inasmuch as this apartment considers a white-wash brush and broom
great innovators, and as it is used by the darkeys for a dormitory,
laundry, drawing-room, nursery, and a cook-room for all, both
whites and blacks, I shall not attempt a detailed description, but
simply refer the reader to Mrs. Harriet Beecher Stowe's accurately
executed daguerreotypes of this southern "institution," given in her
account of Miss Ophelia's exploring and purging expedition to Aunt
Dinah's apartment. (*Uncle Tom*, pages 80, 81.)

My host being leader of the colored class, I took pleasure in occasionally accompanying him and leading the class, and we frequently had uproarious times. In addressing these sable sons and
daughters of the Most High, I termed them brothers and sisters;
but the good brother told me he did not apply these filial and frater-
nal terms to the members of his colored class; he did not think it
proper! Said I, "What do you call them, brother?" "Well, I
call them aunts, uncles, Tom, Dick, or Harry!" reminding me of the
words of Clement the IVth, who having ascended the papal chair,
returned the bow of the congratulating ambassadors and others.

When the master of ceremonies told his Holiness that he should not have returned their salute, "Oh! I beg your pardon," said he, "I have not been Pope long enough to forget good manners."

But, Mr. Editor, it came to pass, in the travel of time, that your humble correspondent and his family moved to the parsonage, provided by the munificence of the circuit. It was a large country house, situated in the centre of an extensive farm, the plantation being tilled by slaves. A part of them were owned by a steward of the circuit. The colored people occupied that nondescript apartment, the quarter, or kitchen, attached to the house; they were allowanced, as it is technically termed here, that is, lived by the steelyards; with the abuse of abundance they could not be charged.

Their magnificent, may I not say princely entertainment, for a fortnight, consisted of one peck unsifted corn meal, ten pounds of pork, or rather rancid bacon, and one quart of molasses. Often have I seen those negroes, property, too, of that wealthy Methodist, work in the sultry sun till 12 o'clock at noon, and then come to the kitchen to mix and cook their chicken feed for dinner, and on bended knees, from my wife would beg a little salt. Their bed-chamber was a strange scene of dirt, confusion, and solitude; black with the smoke of burnt pine knots, strewn with rags and the plucked feathers of stolen chickens. The bed consisted of a few rotten rags spread on a soft plank, and a few more tatters for covering; but, as these people seldom remove their clothing when they retire, they have not so great a demand for counterpanes.

I drew some comfort from the thought that those cases were extreme, and seldom paralleled; but a pious and very wealthy member of one of the churches on the circuit gave me a special invitation to return from church with him, as he wished to converse with me. As we entered his house, he informed me that one of his colored girls had gone to church, got "shouting happy," and had returned in a trance; or at least, her powers of locomotion seemed destroyed, and she had not done any work for two days. He wished me to see her, and pass an opinion on her case. I accompanied him to the kitchen loft, and there my unsophisticated eye saw the same kind of entertainment that I had witnessed before. Since then, I have learned to wonder at nothing of this sort. On passing along the road, I had frequently seen a very aged colored man, a complete cripple, trying to make baskets. I found that his lower limbs were quite useless; his house was like a pigsty, for it was simply a pen of rough, unhewn logs, without window, and but one room; and when the reader is told that this 12 by 18 mansion accommodated two families, and recollects the propensity of the darkeys for the accumulation of rags, he will conclude with me that the interior of this splendid edifice baffles all description. But in just such homes do tens of thousands of negroes in the South live, both free and bond. As I entered, said I, "How are you, uncle?" "I'se bad 'nuff, massa." "Are you free?" "Yes, massa." "Were you always free?" "Ah! no." "How long were you in bondage?" "Fifty years, massa." "Well, what has crippled you so?" "Hard work, an' long at it." "Whom did you belong to?" I was struck with surprise at his answer. A ——— of my circuit, a man of wealth and influence. "Why, you can't work, uncle?" "Must do it, massa." So, slipping a silver coin into his hand, and commending him to the care of his Heavenly Father, I took my leave, and for the present do the same with my reader.

JUNIUS.

LETTER III.

Mr. Editor: Resuming my narrative where I concluded, I would state that, owing to the operation of causes that, to say the least, do not reflect any credit on Southern hospitality, your obedient servant concluded to suspend housekeeping during the winter, and board, a brother having thrown open his doors for our accommodation. This gentleman, like most other property-holders, owned slaves. We frequently held conversations on the subject of slavery, and, as usual, he had no objection to define his position; and his position is the status of every master and slavedriver whose opinion I have ever heard expressed. "O yes, slavery is a great evil; we would be better off without these slaves. But"—yes, that little disjunctive has an awful significance, a barrier more difficult to surmount than the Sierra Nevada. "Well, sir, why are you connected with it? You are a man of position and fortune; why not give the weight of your influence on the side of freedom and humanity?" "Slave labor is more available than free." "It is a terrible evil, then, and yet a question of mere availability!"

On one occasion, I found a little black girl employed as waiting-maid, in fact a general convenience. She seemed like an inoffensive, timid creature. A severe snow-storm arrived about the same time we did, and the weather was fearfully cold. "Hett" must with dispatch execute all orders, whether issued by her master of forty, or her master of four years of age. Her wearing apparel consisted of two garments. Frequently have I seen her ankle deep in the snow, with neither shoes nor stockings on. Hett fell heir to all the supernumerary shoes of the family, great and small; and when, from long service to others they became superannuated, it was her fortune to be destitute. Her suffering condition appealing to my sympathies, on condition of her performing a small job, I promised to purchase her a pair of shoes. But this proposition seemed to arouse the dormant humanity of his majesty, her liege lord, and he procured her a pair. Taking a walk unexpectedly on the lawn in the rear of the house, I found poor Hett "getting it good," as it is termed, with a large-sized hoop-pole. I quietly returned, not having any special preference for such spectacles. One day Hett came to my room, to receive my orders as usual, when upon looking up I found a frightful gash in her cheek. Said I, "What is the matter?" She hung her head, and refused to answer, but on being pressed, and assured that no danger would follow, she replied: "Massa." "Where was it done?" "In the barn."

I felt indignant that such a looking object should have been permitted to enter my room. A few mornings subsequently I saw barefooted Hett come from the barn with a bleeding face, followed by her master. As the kind-hearted brother approached, I inquired if it was he that had struck her in the face. "Don't know," was the answer. I replied, "You ought to know."

Some time subsequently my soul was sickened at the sight of her forehead laid open for an inch and a half in length, and penetrating to the skull. I determined to investigate the matter, and found that a whipping was the cause of the wound, and not by the lash. Her gracious master, attempting to chastise her while standing on the ice, she, in an effort to dodge the blow, fell and struck her head.

On another occasion, seeing bareheaded Hett going in the direction of the barn, and feeling a gush of chivalry, I resolved on an attempt at knight-errantry. But to get a drubbing did not happen to be her errand on that occasion, so I lost my opportunity of becoming a second Moses, by delivering a captive from her Egyptian taskmaster's cruelty. Poor Hett! I have devoutly prayed that she might soon die, for death can be her only deliverer.

Rev. J. D. Long's *Pictures of Slavery* have been denounced as very erroneous, and he has been charged with misrepresenting both master and slave. Well, we cannot all "see eye to eye," but I think the most, if not all of his positions are correct, and I could substantiate them by an abundance of facts that cannot lie.

I have made attempts at catechizing the juvenile woolly heads, with the following results. That there must be exceptions, all will admit.

"Well, Getty, how are you?" "Right smart." "Do you say your prayers?" "Umph." (A negative.) "Don't your mistress teach you?" "Umph." "Well, who made you?" "Dunno, 'spect mammy." "Don't you know who made all things, the earth, the sky, and the sea?" "'Spect they cummed."

Taking tea, on a certain Sabbath evening, at the house of my former host, the cook they had employed the last year entered the kitchen weeping, wringing her hands, and sobbing out that "her master had sold her to 'Georgy,' and she must go next Tuesday, and leave four of her children;" six children she claimed, though she never claimed to be a wife. She besought us, "for God's sake, to buy her." I now looked to the brow of our steward for a cloud of indignation, and to his lips for some innuendo, at least, against slavery. He struck up a merry tune, and told his wife that he had heard glorious accounts of the far South; it was a perfect paradise for slaves—and on he sung. Whether the poor woman went to Georgia or not, I am unable to say, but not long after a chained captive was seen on the deck of a vessel bound down the river.

Our county court-house being not far distant, and hearing that a sale was to take place there in the afternoon, I concluded to attend.

After a number of articles were disposed of, I saw a simultaneous movement towards the jail, and moving with the mass, I soon found myself before an auctioneer, standing in the door of the jail, and presently saw what was to be done. Casting my eyes up to the prison's grated window, I saw an old woman, sixty years of age. Her countenance presented the most awful spectacle of horror that ever met my astonished gaze; her eyes were swollen, her features distorted, and from every pore seemed to stream unearthly terror. She being old and ugly, was not brought down for the examination of buyers.

Article No. 2 was a man fifty years old; he, like the old woman, was not exposed to the gaze of the crowd. He was sold for $200.

2

Chattel No. 3 was a mother, thirty-eight years of age, with pain painted on every feature of her face, trembling with agitation, and sobbing aloud, while a fine little boy clung to her bosom, and shrunk away, as the kind and considerate crier attempted to grasp him. Taking hold of the little fellow below the knees, he held him up at arms' length, swaying him to and fro, and crying, " How much ? how much ?" He was sold; the price I do not recollect.

The mother followed next.

Article No. 5 was a fine, plump, sleek girl of sixteen. One of the nigger-buyers, a good-looking, young, unmarried man, seemed struck; his fingers were busy exploring the interior of her mouth, rubbing her ivories, pinching her arms, feeling her sides, and, indeed, thoroughly trying the solidity of her muscle; she brought $990.

Article No. 6 was not present; a certificate from a physician stated that he was lying dangerously ill with the typhoid fever; he must be bought at a venture. A number bid, and he was soon knocked off.

There were some twelve or fourteen in the lot; I concluded I had seen enough to prove that this is an age of progress, and that this sight of 1857 reflects immortal renown on the civilization and Christianity of the 19th century.

JUNIUS.

LETTER IV.

February 3, 1858.

MR. EDITOR : Having in my last communication given you a description of some scenes I witnessed at a public vendue, you may presume that Southern sentiment generally is averse to the system that produces such fearful results. Perhaps I cannot better illustrate the sentiments of the South, than by detailing a conversation I had a few days since with a man of color. He told me that his master died when he (a slave) was fifteen years of age, that he was sold to meet pressing liabilities, and having served his new master and mistress until their death, he became free. For his first wife he married a slave belonging to ——; that —— sold his wife and a part of his children South. Said I, " Why did you not marry a free girl?" " I was guine to, massa, but massa told me he put me in his pocket (that is, sell him to the South), if I married a free girl."

And lest, Mr. Editor, you should suppose that man is ranked as a moral monster among the good people of this vicinity, I will state that he recently died, and that the following is his obituary, as published in a paper. I give it *verbatim et literatim et punctuatim :* "—— was a sincere and devoted friend, unwilling to acknowledge a fault in those he esteemed, a kind and affectionate husband and parent, and a most indulgent and considerate master. His heart was filled with benevolence for the poor, and his hand was ever ready to serve them, and he often risked his property to favor a friend. Brave, generous, hospitable, and kind, even in his dying hours, can surviving friendship do else than hope, there is a mansion prepared for him in that house not made with hands, eternal in the heavens ?"

And now, if you will permit, I will review some of the positions taken by Rev. J. D. Long, in his *Pictures of Slavery*, which, according to the redoubtable Rev. Dr. Thomas Jefferson Quigley, are the head and front of his offending.

First, Rev. J. D. Long is charged, pages 43, 44, 45 of his book, with misrepresenting the Philadelphia Conference and the border difficulties. In proof of what he (J. D. Long) asserts, he appeals to the memorable documents published on pages 41 and 42 of his book ; and after reading that paper, and comparing it with the Discipline and Doctrines of the M. E. Church, South, struck with the identity of the two, we are forced to exclaim—

"Strange there should such a difference be
'Twixt tweedledum and tweedledee."

Again he is charged with the same offence on page 328, where he states that preachers hold slaves indirectly. If none of the members of the Philadelphia Conference hold slaves in the manner there hinted, we are slightly mistaken ; and if application is not made at the ensuing session of the Philadelphia Conference, for admission, by one of these slaveholders, then again we are " slightly mistaken." " How did they acquire slave property," do you ask ? I will illustrate : In conversation with a gentleman recently, I asked the question, " How did a certain man become possessed of so much property ?" The reply was, " He married it." Can the reader make the application ?

And Mr. Long further asks, " How inconsistent it is in the Philadelphia and Baltimore Conferences to forbid their members to hold slaves, when they suffer them to be held by exhorters and class-leaders ?" And he might have added local preachers, for one of the lay stewards of the Philadelphia Conference was a local preacher, and if I am not again "slightly mistaken," a slaveholder. And among the stewards of a certain circuit, not a hundred miles from T. J. Quigley, are held at least thirty slaves. In conversation with an exhorter a short time since, he told me the reason why he bought a slave was because they paid a better interest than hirelings. So much for the first specification.

Specification second, "Misrepresenting the people of Maryland and Delaware;" first, on page 13. How misrepresentation is found on that page I am not able to say. Mr. Long simply asks: "If slavery shall be found to be a great crime against God and humanity in these States (Maryland and Delaware), what must it be in its most aggravated manifestation?" But as Rev. Thomas Jefferson Quigley has recently been made a D. D., perhaps that has sharpened his perceptive faculties. Next, page 39 is charged as misrepresentation. Mr. Long says: "This book (i. e., *Pictures of Slavery*) will banish me from my relatives, from the graves of my honored parents, and from my native State. If I were to visit my former places of residence, I might not receive personal violence; but the man who should entertain me would be marked, and would have to suffer on my account."

We shall see whether this be false. In conversation recently with a relative of J. D. Long, he told me "he was exceedingly sorry that John D. had written that book; that he had effectually excluded himself from southern territory." And a good Methodist politely told the writer that "Long ought to be treated, and would be if he showed himself here, to a coat of tar and feathers." And a very considerate Methodist lady told me, that "any member of the Philadelphia Conference that would not vote for the expulsion of J. D. Long, should never preach on the Eastern Shore." I loaned this book to an exhorter, and he returned it with this learned criticism: "The book is a tissue of nonsense; its doctrines are most ludicrous; if they are carried out, we shall have to admit the colored people to an equality with us, and call them brother and sister; and what would the world think of us?" I might touch a little nearer home if I chose, but I forbear.

But for a complete overthrow of the objections to page 39, let any reader turn to the notices of the press, as published in the latter part of Mr. Long's book, page 9, and read the sentiments of the Easton (Md.) *Star*. Page 40 is also appealed to, to sustain the second specification; but we are as much at a loss to determine where

Rev. Dr. Thomas Jefferson Quigley finds fallacy there as on page 13, unless Rev. Thomas Jefferson Quigley charges Mr. Long with downright lying; for on the page Mr. Long simply narrates a conversation he held with a friend, and that friend's answer; then an avowal of determination on the part of Mr. Long to wage an uncompromising warfare against the sin of slavery. Perhaps the misrepresentation consists in this "*sin* of slavery." Dr. Quigley had better turn to Discipline, page 212. But perhaps the Discipline merely means "a physical evil," and a physical evil may not be a sin; therefore, according to Discipline, slavery is not a sin, and Mr. Long misrepresents in calling it a sin. Or it may be that Dr. Quigley charges the expressed determination of Mr. Long, "to wage perpetual warfare against slavery" as false; if so, the future course of Mr. Long must determine that fact. If the last hypothesis be correct, I will ask, may not the same charge be preferred against one more member of one of the Border Conferences? More anon.

JUNIUS.

LETTER V.

March 10, 1858.

MR. EDITOR: With your kind permission, I will pay my respects to Dr. Quigley and Rev. J. D. Long once more. The next page mentioned in specification 2d, is p. 57. Mr. Long says, on this page: "Things have come to that point now that slaveholders want to know your sentiments soon after you arrive on your circuit." This is the only statement on page 57 that can be the supposed misrepresentation. To show that this is a correct representation, and no *mis* about it, permit me to state facts: About a fortnight after my arrival on this circuit, necessity impelled me to take a stage ride; the driver, a red-faced, burly man, a slaveholder, seemed exceedingly anxious for a confab. Feeling in rather a meditative mood, the conversation was nearly all on one side, and his questions were replied to by monosyllables. At last he said: "Mr. ———, you are our new preacher, I believe? How many Conferences are there? How far does your Conference extend? Well, a division occurred some time ago in the M. E. Church. I have understood that it was divided not on a question of doctrine, but on the subject of slavery. I think it would have been better had the Eastern Shore gone with the Church South. Some of these Northern preachers and people have most ridiculous notions of slavery—what is your opinion?" Thus he went on, trying the pumping process most energetically; but, perhaps, not effectually.

A wealthy member of our church who, as I understand, holds the opinion that negroes are a link between the orang outang and the human being, that they have no souls, and consequently are not accountable, asked me if I thought slavery was " of the Lord ?" I replied that I thought it had quite an opposite origin. An exhorter inquired if I did not think slavery was right? But it is quite unnecessary to specify instances.

Mr. Long further says: " If the preacher confesses his anti-slavery principles, he must leave, or be annoyed all the time." I will make short work with this "misrepresentation," by simply challenging Dr. Quigley to preach on my circuit, or on his own, an anti-slavery sermon. I have class-leaders, stewards, exhorters, local preachers, white and black, that hold slaves. Now I defy him to come to my circuit and execute the rule of discipline found on page 213. And he need not endeavor to screen himself behind the assertion that "the laws do not admit of emancipation, and permit the liberated slave to enjoy freedom !" We assert they do, and demand proof to the contrary. Even admitting that the *laws* are opposed to emancipation, the doctor knows, or ought to know, that custom is stronger than law. Annually hundreds of colored people are manumitted in this State.

The law, Mr. Editor (omitting its verbiage), is simply this, according to the statute-book and the teaching of an ex-member of Congress: The clerk, during the tenure of whose office the bill of emancipation is filed, is required to communicate to the Colonization Society the fact of the slave's emancipation ; and he then becomes subject to their demand. But now mark, for here is the broken arm of the law: If the Board of Managers make a requisition on the negro, and he refuse to obey, it is made the duty of the sheriff of the county to remove him from the State ; but the Board of Managers do not make the demand (officially), therefore it is not the duty of the county officers to remove him, and his freedom attaches to him, and he cannot be removed; so, in the language of a gentleman of the bar, "there is no legal impediment in the path of full emancipation." But, admitting the law to place an absolute veto on manumission, the members of the evangelical churches have it in their power to alter or annul any law in the statute-book.

Mr. Long further says: "And if the General Conference should ever make non-slaveholding, and non-slavebreeding a test of membership, the Eastern Shore of Maryland will go to the Church South."

Well, I have yet to find the man or Methodist with whom I have conversed, that has not expressed the same opinions precisely; and many contend that it should have gone with the great Southern secession.

Page 73 is next referred to. Mr. Long there says: "What a mad dog is in a crowded thoroughfare, what a heretic is in Spain, what a republican is in Russia, the abolitionist is in the slave States."

The reader will bear witness that in these papers I have scarcely uttered a single opinion, but merely stated facts, and left others to reason and opinionate; let me adduce a few more, to throw some light on this point of the investigation: Shortly after my arrival on this field of labor, in company with some Methodists, I hinted my opinion in regard to the darling institution; they communicated to me very plainly and positively, that such sentiments in this part of the world might do for a man's bosom, but never for his tongue. Said I, "Do we not here enjoy freedom of speech?" "Yes, so long as your speech pleases the people!"

A letter recently appeared in *Zion's Herald* from Delaware, over the signature of J. Pasterfield. It came under the eye of a number of his friends; of course it was universally denounced as bombast; but mark the wisdom of their conjectures in regard to the design of the missive: The verdict of all, and they were not a few, was, that "he is tired of the Eastern Shore, and his purpose is, by the utterance of these incendiary sentiments, to exile himself from the South; he wants to go up." What a volume of meaning in the conjecture of his friends! Allow me to say that if Mr. Long wants to prove the truth of his own remarks, let him pay a visit to the old Ferry over the Pocomoke, and we will have a living, or perhaps a *dead* demonstration. But I will allow a third party to decide this part of the controversy. If Mr. Long will place his book in the hands of the president of a life insurance company, and then announce his determination to visit the South, and the company issue a policy, then we will consider the representation of Mr. Long a false one. Perhaps the following, clipped from the Cambridge paper, may explain the sensitiveness of the South.

MOVEMENTS IN DORCHESTER.

At a meeting of the people of Dorchester County, held in Cambridge, on the 2d of November, to take into consideration the better protection of the interests of slaveowners, among other things that were done, it was resolved to enforce the various acts of assembly against all persons for buying corn, wheat, and other article prohibited by law, and otherwise trading and dealing with slaves, without an order from their masters, and to enforce rigidly the act of 1715, chap. 44, relative to servants and slaves ; and all owners who do not wish to incur the penalties of said law are hereby notified to keep their servants and slaves at home or furnish them written passes, when sent beyond the limits prescribed by law, as they will surely be arrested and placed in custody.

The act of 1715, chap. 44, sec. 2d, provides that "from and after the publication thereof, no servant or servants whatever in this province, either by indenture, or by the custom of the counties, or hired for wages, shall travel by land or water ten miles from the house of his, or her, or their master, mistress or dame, without a note under their hands, or under the hand of his, her, or their overseer, under the penalty of being taken up for a runaway, and to suffer such penalty as hereafter provided against runaways." The act of 1806, chap. 81, sec. 5th, provides that any person taking up such runaways shall have and receive six dollars, to be paid by the master or owner. It was also determined to have put in force the act of 1825, chap. 161, and the act of 1839, chap. 320, relative to idle, vagabond, free negroes, providing for their sale, or banishment from the State. All persons interested are hereby notified that the aforesaid law in particular will be enforced, and all officers failing to enforce them will be presented to the grand jury; and those who desire to avoid the penalties of the aforesaid statutes, are requested to conform to those provisions.

Published by order of Committee of Vigilance.

In connection with which, insert the following paragraph from a Baltimore paper :—

"STAMPEDE OF SLAVES.—On the night of the 24th ult., twenty-eight slaves made their escape from Cambridge, Md. A reward of $3100 has been offered by some of the owners for the recovery of the runaways. These make forty-two who have left that place within two weeks."

Among the number are twelve belonging to a circuit steward of the M. E. Church.

The slaves of Egypt had their Moses; the crushed thousands of the West Indies had their Wilberforce ; the degraded vassals of Hayti baptized with blood the hour of their terrible triumph ; and there is still a God who has said, " Vengeance is mine !" *Plus ultra.*

JUNIUS.

LETTER VI.

MR. LONG'S BOOK VERIFIED.

MR. EDITOR: In taking another glance at the specifications, in the charges preferred by Dr. Quigley against Rev. J. D. Long, I find page 89 next comes under his frown.

Mr. Long says : " Very little provision is made for the education of the poor." If Dr. Quigley deems this incorrect, I would refer him, for information, to the late message of the retiring Governor Ligon, of Maryland; and as to Mr. Long's description of a school-house, on the same page, I have seen such things in reality, times innumerable. Further, on the same page: " There is not much difficulty in the South in raising money for a barbecue, or to buy whiskey for political purposes ; but when funds are wanted to buy a library, that is quite another question." Mr. Editor, you are a critic ; can you see any misrepresentation there ? Do we not know that raising money for a barbecue and for a library are different matters ? This is all Mr. Long asserts; but, allowing that he wished to convey the impression that it is more difficult to procure money to purchase a library, than to purchase rum for political purposes, in illustration even of this view, allow me to say, that not 100 miles from the parish of Dr. Quigley is a circuit on which is one Sabbath School that continues in operation three months of the year—and not a circulating book belonging to the institution ; and belonging to the circuit was a steward, who, according to his own confession, spent $1000 during one campaign for political purposes. And in another vineyard of the Lord, embracing a district of 250 square miles, was a circulating library of 142 books; and one political party, if we may rely on the word of a member of that party, spent $3000 in one season for the purpose of influencing voters. Facts of this sort, not fancies, press on our attention with painful force and frequency. I cannot but think it unfortunate for the Doctor and his cause, that he should have placed this chapter on the controverted list; for I am fearful that his objections to its truth may start a train of investigation that will result most disastrously to the cause it was intended to sustain. It is a most unpleasant performance to institute invidious comparisons, and I beg leave to be excused from the task on this occasion, simply referring the reader to the revelations of the U. S. Census for 1850; compare the persons over 20 years of age, unable to read or write, in the Southern, with the same number, *pro rata*, in the Northern States; compare the slaveholding district in the Philadelphia Conference with the non-slaveholding districts, in regard to financial and educational progress.

Pages 90, 91, are also false, according to the dictum of the prosecutor; but, as Mr. Long here merely relates a matter of personal experience, we are unwilling to be an accuser of the brethren, but shall consider the words of Mr. Long as much entitled to credence as the *dixit* of Dr. Quigley. In the same category is page 173; in this chapter Mr. Long simply discusses the effect of spirituous drinks on the negroes—he affirms that "rum brutalized the slave" (stupendous misrepresentation!). Might he not have added, and the master likewise? "And destroys his desire for liberty; for whenever a slave becomes reconciled to his condition, he ceases to have any moral character much beyond a brute." Perhaps, as the principles involved in this proposition are more of a metaphysical than physical character, the learned Doctor is more competent to pass on the subject than plain J. D. Long and his humble defender. We will surrender our judgment—as the superior mind should always rule. This page contains the assertion that "honesty in a slave is not valued for its own sake, but in the light of its pecuniary advantage." I will here frankly affirm, that I cannot underwrite this opinion; but, lest it may be supposed that we think there is no truth in the assumption, please take a case in point: During 1857, a member of the M. E. Church, whose laudatory obituary appeared in the "great official," having died intestate, a black man belonging to the estate of the deceased, a Methodist also, was put on the block by the executors, and purchased by a colored local preacher on the same circuit. A short period after his purchase, the same piece of property decamped, as rumor says, owing to harsh treatment. He was apprehended, returned, taken to Baltimore, and offered to the Southern market, but his sale was spoiled by the constant assertion of the negro that his family connections, together with himself, was subject to fits; information that was perfectly correct. As far as we could learn, commiseration seemed to be felt for the local preacher.

Again, on the same page is an assertion, and some proof of its truth. The proposition is—"As a general thing, masters would rather have their slaves drunk occasionally, than constantly sober, thoughtful, and religious." Proof—"Hence, when there is any rumor of an insurrection, preachers are warned to stop their religious meetings, but no warning is given to the retailers of whiskey not to sell to the slaves." Mr. Long says: "We know this from painful experience." Bold is he that will question the experience of another, yet the Doctor has done it. Well, a most terrible damnation awaits Mr. Long, for another John says that "all liars shall have their part in the lake which burneth with fire and brimstone"—unless the Doctor, along with a good many others, thinks that assertion of the older John is a "misrepresentation." Page 174 next comes under the prosecutor's orthodox scalpel. Mr. Long says: "Where slavery abounds, education is below par." We should not have challenged that position had we been the Doctor, but, "Where ignorance is bliss, 'tis folly to be wise." We again beg to be excused from making the unkind comparison. And further, that the seller of rum is more respected than the school-teacher." Again we cannot underwrite the author's sentiment, but a fact may not be unacceptable. Within a radius of half a mile from the spot on which I write, there are ten places where "liquid fire and distilled damnation" is sold, and two establishments devoted to the sale of that article exclusively; and in the same territory there are two schools. The rumseller carries on his business all the year; seven-eighths of all the schools in the State, during a part of the year, suspend; the community gives a handsome support to the rumseller; but from $150 to $200 is the average salary paid to the rural school-teacher; and as a consequence, in Maryland one person in every thirteen is unable to read or write; while in that "hotbed of abolitionism," Massachusetts, but one in every thirty-five is in the same pitiable predicament.

Mr. Long further says: "Chattel slavery inevitably begets idleness, ignorance, and licentiousness." Facts and figures that cannot misrepresent, might be adduced to substantiate this affirmation, but charity forbids me to lift the veil. I will simply say that a member of the Baltimore Conference made the same assertion before a Virginian audience, when a vote of leave of absence was tendered him forthwith. And the venerable John Hersey, arriving at the same conclusion that Mr. Long does, told a Southern congregation that they were "trying to climb to heaven with a nigger on one shoulder and a barrel of whiskey on the other."

Page 232 is next noticed by the Doctor, but we here avow that it is beneath our dignity to pry so piercingly, or judge so harshly; and if a Doctor of Divinity be driven to such pitiable extremes to find an occasion of offence against the sentiment of a Christian brother, we know not whether to pity or despise him. The last page mentioned in this specification is 394. Mr. Long, speaking of an infernal monster which he had just described, says: "He could have robbed as many quadroon girls of their virtue as he wanted, and the laws of Maryland were powerless to harm him." Why, in the first place, the crime would have been a deed of darkness, known to none but the villain and his victim; had the quadroon told her tale of ruin in the neighborhood, it would have been stigmatized as " nigger news." Had she appealed to the law, Maryland justice would have responded: " The testimony of a colored person cannot be received against a white." Mr. Long declares: " Had I gone to your court-house and publicly preached against the wickedness of those laws, a public meeting of saints and sinners, moralists and blackguards, would soon have been called," etc. Now the misrepresentation, we think, consists in saying that such a meeting would have been *called*. They would not have waited for an invitation. Though most of us are Methodists, we will own up to our Calvinist brethren that such a speech would be an " *effectual call*."

Really, Mr. Editor, in all sober earnestness, we are firmly of opinion that Mr. Long, here, at least, is more sinned against than sinning, and that a charge of misrepresenting the people of Maryland ought to be preferred against his attorneyship, the reverend prosecutor; for he must certainly know that *he* cannot publicly, or with boldness, privately, on the Eastern Shore, denounce the laws that support and sanctify slavery. Oh! he may tell us " all things are possible; but all things are not expedient!" We throw down the gauntlet, and challenge the Doctor to take it up.

And now, for the first time, almost, perhaps I may have the temerity to express an opinion concerning the Doctor, though it may precipitate the painful penalty of ecclesiastical decapitation.

[The opinion which followed, and which was published in this letter, we deemed irrelevant and personal, and omitted it here.] Adieu.

P. S.—A fugitive slave has just arrived, and the town seems all agog. I will go and take a look at his " smiling face." Again adieu.

JUNIUS.

LETTER VII.

March 17, 1858.

MR. EDITOR: Still pursuing the circuitous path of Rev. Dr. Quigley, in his precipitate pursuit of Rev. J. D. Long, we arrive at page 227: "You must not even dare to hint," says the book, "that it is wrong in America to strip a woman and cowhide her, because she is restless under slavery." Does the Doctor, by declaring this chapter contraband, mean to maintain that women are never cowhided in Maryland by their masters? A devoted Methodist, recently in the presence of the writer, was dilating upon the thorough and efficacious cowhiding he had given his black woman, for refusing patiently to submit to a thrashing from her indignant mistress! While listening to the recital, my blood boiled a little, but suddenly cooled down lower than zero, upon recollecting that our church is "conservative," and that "agitation is much to be deplored," it being peculiarly offensive to doctors. Not being skilled in the nice science of casuistry, I will not assume the province of determining whether or not some remote, mystified idea of self-preservation had not some influence in sealing my silence. But if Dr. Quigley thinks I have proved recreant to duty, I will give the brother's name, and turn over the case to him; here will be a fine opportunity for the Doctor to give the church a practical proof that Mr. Long misrepresents.

Upon the alleged misrepresentation of the ministers who have labored in Maryland and Delaware, a hoary-headed sage of the Philadelphia Conference said: "Old as I am, my lips are hermetically sealed, and as to Bro. Long's book, I see no misrepresentations." We now propose to review the objections included in specification 4th: "Misrepresenting the members of the M. E. Church." First, page 48: "By actual slaveholders, I mean those who hold them for gain, just as the irreligious hold them." So that is a false statement, if the showing of the Doctor be correct; but he would have arrived at an entirely different conclusion, had he been present, and listened to the discussion of this subject, that occurred a brief period since. It was there warmly maintained, by a circuit steward, that he did not pretend to hold his slaves for any other purpose whatsoever than a mercenary purpose, if by mercenary is meant for hire or gain; and he was utterly unable to understand the speech of Rev. J. A. Collins, delivered at the late General Conference, in which he asserted that there is little or no mercenary slaveholding in the church. Indeed, in this particular, the South is under no obligations to Dr. Quigley, and do not thank him for the attempt to clear them of the charges of pro-slavery tendencies. This is one exception to his universal popularity; but we are told there are spots even on the sun. As to the statement of the number of slaves held by members of the M. E. Church, I do not think it at all extravagant. A certain church, on a certain circuit, numbering only one hundred members, will furnish one-sixtieth of that number; multiply every one hundred members in the slaveholding district by fifty, and see the product.

On page 49, the author drops a remark that we cannot underwrite, and one we do not believe: "All these (mercenary slaveholders) are sheltered by the Discipline of our church." The Discipline of our church does not shelter them; it is the evasions of the Discipline that protect them; for we aver that the chapter on slavery is a dead letter, an effete thing, defunct, beyond all hope of resurrection.

Page 52 is regarded, I presume, as a most terrible aspersion upon us Southern saints; listen to Mr. Long: "Tell it not in Papal Rome, that Methodists, in the 19th century, in the United States of America, are contending that a portion of the human race should be kept in ignorance, that the grogshop is better than the school-house, and rum better than education." Suppose we walk right up to this assumption, view it with a critic's eye, and reason a little upon it, on the syllogistic plan:—

The institutions of a community usually embody the wishes, feelings, and designs of that community.

There are institutions in the South devoted to the manufacture and sale of intoxicating liquor, but none to the education of the people of color. Therefore, it is according to the wishes, feeling, and design of the South that rum be preferred to education.

Within my knowledge, there is not on the Eastern Shore a school, secular or Sabbath, for the improvement of the children of color. It may be said that our churches are seminaries, and there at least they may learn the science of salvation. It is true, and for this spiritual tuition they are willing to pay quite handsomely.

We next notice page 226: "Preachers who insist on a strict moral life, on dealing justly in business transactions, and being truthful in words, and self-denying in our lives, and liberal according to the ability God has given us, are greatly undervalued among us." We are afraid, Mr. Editor, that the same remarks will apply to other meridians more northern than the meridian of Maryland; for flesh-flattering and sin-soothing strains are highly acceptable to the modern mighty, who still repel the faithful prophet, as "mine enemy." "I have always found it easier to get up a shout than a Bible class." Amen! My heart responds; for I have "got up" many a shout, and made an attempt to "get up" a Bible class, and did "get up" one—having purchased a number of question books at my own expense, and "got up" a young men's prayer meeting, but had to get them down again, for complaints were made that the expense of illumination (burning two lamps for an hour) was more than the church could endure. So the Bible class and prayer meeting went by the board, but the shout still goes on!

The fact that Mr. Long wishes to prove on the following page is simply this: that slavery deprecates and denounces agitation, delights in and demands the syren's soothing song of sweet tranquillity; that it would place an everlasting quietus upon discussion, muzzling the mouth of the pulpit, the press and the people, all of which we cordially indorse.

The last page alluded to in this specification is page 385: "Within the last seven years a member of the M. E. Church of the highest standing made a will, by which he left his slaves to be sold at auction to the highest bidder! This act was regarded as a shrewd business transaction by the community in which he lived, and was not thought to reflect the slightest on his Christian character; the newspaper eulogized his virtues in an extravagant manner." We pronounce this narrative true, or a downright lie. About such facts the author could not be mistaken; and I have no doubt he could have added many instances of a similar character. If he could not, I can. A little more than a twelvemonth since, a member of the M. E. Church died, having left a slave, whom another Methodist sold to a nigger-buyer. Another died within a shorter period of time, and his two-legged cattle were sold along with his four-legged. A Methodist owned a slave girl that was receiving the attention of a colored man: he worked hard, lived economically, and bought this girl for a wife; he took a bill of sale, and filed a deed of manumission the same day. That slave never cost that Methodist master one cent; he got her by inheritance; her splendid moral, spiritual and literary education devolved upon the shoulders of others; for, be it understood, that she graduated with distinguished honors at the most eminent literary institution for the people of color south of Mason and Dixon's Line (her alma mater was the kitchen!), yet when this honorable, high-minded negro man wanted a companion, he had to pay hundreds of dollars to a Methodist master for her. Does Dr. Quigley want the names of the parties for the purpose of instituting disciplinary proceedings, he can have them. Or does he design to prosecute Junius for "misrepresentation?"

We now come to notice the last specification of this immortalized charge, viz., "misrepresenting the colored people." Poor creatures! how unkind and unchristian it is to misuse them; but that ingrate, J. D. Long, has been guilty of the overwhelmingly amazing crime of misrepresenting them. Certainly, if there is one flame in the fire infernal more intensely hot than another, J. D. Long shall have it.

Page 20 comes first in the series: " I have never known of more than one white minister of the gospel who has performed religious service at the funeral of the slave." I add, neither have I. There is nothing else on the page that could be distorted into misrepresentation.

On page 20 the brow of the Doctor seems to gather portentous wrath. We deem this the most important chapter of the entire book, and would advise the readers of the *Herald* to spend a dollar in the purchase of this book—this page is well worth the amount. The only statement that we can possibly imagine that the Doctor thinks overdrawn is this—Mr. Long, speaking of the bright mulatto girl, says: "For them there is no virtue after a certain age." To illustrate and confirm this view, I could tell a tale of most terrible truth, and to this depth of degradation (Oh! tell it not in Gath) they are driven by the lash of their master. I have heard the young Virginian master boast of the number of his conquests of this kind! But I forbear; I am afraid to trust my pen; my temples throb, when I recollect what I have seen and heard. Fearing that the facts I have at command would be totally unfit for a high-toned journal, as the *Herald*, I leave the public to rely on the assertion without the proof.

The objections to page 383 are entirely too trifling for notice. If you, Mr. Editor, or the Doctor himself, will pay us a visit, we will show the reality, of which page 383 is a true and graphic picture.

And now, as I am about to take an affectionate leave of the Doctor, and his prosecution, allow a concluding remark: 1. I have not written for the purpose of giving publicity to my views on the subject of slavery; I have studiously avoided presenting my opinion or indulging in declamation. I may take a future opportunity to give my opinion upon the great question now shaking the American nation. 2. Neither has it been my object to blindly sustain all the positions taken by Rev. J. D. Long, in his work on slavery; but seeing that he seemed to stand solitary and alone, a target for the artillery of the mighty—and small arms of the mean—with scarce a single friend to defend him, and most devoutly believing that his book is a statement of facts, and that he gives a correct view of the position of the M. E. Church in this part of the world, I concluded at all hazards to enter the arena. 3. My object has not been to lampoon Dr. Quigley; I respect him for his Christian and gentle-manly character, but I think him most egregiously mistaken, having committed something worse than a blunder in policy. I would not occupy his position in that day when all wrongs shall be righted, when the oppressed shall be raised, and the oppressor crushed, "when lightning shall scathe and thunder try the soul," for the value of every slave from Delaware to Florida. 4. Neither has the purpose of aspersing the South prompted the part which I have taken. No; remove the curse of slavery, that, like Egyptian midnight, has set-tled down upon the South, annihilate this hydra-headed monster, whose ravages desolate this fair creation, and this shore will rejoice and blossom as the rose, and take her proper position in America's magnificent march of progress. Soon will she attain a pre-eminently proud rank among political powers and religious communities. That that auspicious hour may speedily arrive, is the earnest prayer of

JUNIUS.

It was not long before we found that Junius was exciting some attention, as the following from *Zion's Herald*, will indicate:—

"LETTERS FROM MARYLAND.—We hear, in a roundabout way, that there is a little anxiety at home to find out who "Junius" is, in order to get rid of him. He is responsible. Don't be frightened, friends. If you have any counter evidence to urge, bring it along. The Dark Ages are passing away, and men begin to say what they please."

At this period, we received a letter from J. D. Long, asking "who is Junius?"

As the trial of J. D. Long was to take place at the ensuing session of our Conference, great anxiety was felt by the brethren at Snow

3

Hill concerning the result. His name was associated with all that was mean and abominable. Not one of those so violently opposed to the author of *Pictures of Slavery* had ever seen the cover of his book, much less explored its contents ; but had, we presume, jumped at a conclusion concerning the character of its contents from reading the following editorial in the *Worcester County Shield* (Snow Hill, Maryland), of Feb. 6, 1858, edited by Thomas E. Martin :—

"LITERARY HODGE-PODGE.—A sanctified imbecile, rejoicing in the euphonious cognomen of the '*Reverend*' *John Dixon Long*, has recently been guilty of the absurdity of writing (what he in the plenitude of his idiotic self esteem doubtless considers) a *book ;* and truly, if a conglomeration of the most hypocritical sentiments that ever emanated from any abolition press, and a tissue of the most distorted and palpable misrepresentations, be the requisites for the production of such a literary effort, then is the *book* in question fully entitled to the appellation. A more stupid and slumber-provoking narrative of '*facts* and fancies' it has never been our bad fortune to peruse. The writer apprising his readers, in the outset, that he is of Southern birth, and therefore more worthy of credibility than one 'not to the manor born,' professes to give truthful and graphic ' pictures of Slavery in Church and State,' &c.—more particularly of the system as it exists in Delaware and Maryland. If we are to believe the authenticity of the incidents with which the book is so profusely interspersed, the author must have had rare and abundant opportunities of becoming acquainted with the negro character. But, as we are disposed to be charitably incredulous, we hesitate to adopt the belief that Mr. Long was guilty of the ungrateful meanness of roaming over Southern plantations in the guise of an abolition incendiary, after he had gorged himself to repletion with Southern hospitality. The anecdotes, therefore, he is so fond of lugging in on every opportunity, simply resolve themselves into lies—whether *premeditated* or not rests with his own *conscience*—the pocket interest is doubtless the main object.

"In endeavoring to maintain the negro's capability for acquiring equal intellectual excellence with the white man, our author refers to such low bred blackguards as Fred. Douglass, Wells, Brown, and a few others of like stamp. While we do not accord to these scoundrels any talent above mediocrity, the very fact of their being *mulattoes* instead of the regular Congo, proves the white man's supremacy. The nearer Cuffee resembles the white man in blood and feature, the nearer he approaches to him in intellectual excellence. But admitting, for the sake of argument, that Douglass and such like possesses all the *physical* attributes of the genuine 'Ebo shin,' and that they are gifted with minds as great as the greatest, still, this would prove nothing. As ' one swallow does not make a summer,' so one or a dozen *smart* niggers cannot be considered as a true sample of the whole tribe. It requires no labored argument to prove the Ethiop's vast intellectual inferiority to the white race. History saves us the trouble. From the earliest period down to the present he has been the lowest in the scale of humanity. Left to his own unaided efforts he sinks to a level with the brute. It is only on his acquaintance with the whites that he emerges from his native barbarism. And why is it? Every race of mankind at some period were in a similar state to the present native African. At one period in the world's history the Caucasian was sunk as low as the African. The only answer that suggests itself to the question above propounded is, that the African has been, is, and we venture to assert, ever will be deficient in the possession of that *inventive* genius, and that indomitable will that enable a barbarous people to become an enlightened people. To the possession of these faculties is to be attributed the white man's intellectual superiority.

"In alluding to the disruption in 1844 of the Methodist Episcopal Church into separate ecclesiastical governments, owing to the meddlesome interference of a few hot headed zealots with Southern affairs, the writer exclaims, ' I thank my Divine Redeemer for New England Methodism.' If any faith is to be placed in the reports so prevalent respecting New England's morals and religion, we should think that that section would be the last place to hold up for our edification. *En passant*, the Methodists south of Mason and Dixon's line ought, in our opinion, to secede from that stew of fanaticism and treason, the Northern Conference, if they wish to be regarded as friends to the Union of these United States.

" In the further elucidation of his views respecting slavery, this consistent follower of the pure founder of Christianity has the effrontery to recommend as examples such villains as Freeborn Garretson and Fred. Douglass—the last especially who had the hardihood in a public meeting to denounce the Father of his Country as a *scoundrel*—and this too in the presence of white men calling themselves Americans—oh shame, where is thy blush ! Our opinion of the Reverend nincompoop who could recommend the conduct of such rascals as those above, as being worthy of imitation, is not a very complimentary one. He is evidently one of two things : If sincere in the sentiments he advocates, he is, to use a common expression, a natural fool ; if not, a most detestable hypocrite.

" He willingly concedes a generous disposition to his Southern acquaintances when he says, that ' if' he visited them he would not receive personal violence. He qualifies the concession, however, by stating ' that the man who should entertain him would be marked, and would have to suffer on his account.' We opine, that the Reverend gentleman arrogates to himself more personal importance than he is justly entitled to. The ' generosity' that would scorn to maltreat a '*superannuated*' imbecile, could not totally divest itself of the feelings of scorn and contempt that would naturally attach themselves to a vain and officious intermeddler.

" ' 'Tis an ill bird that befouls its own nest,' is a trite and homely Scottish adage. Should our readers desire to see the truth of the proverb exemplified, we advise them by all means to purchase and read *Pictures of Slavery*, by the *Reverend John Dixon Long*."

The reader will relish the summary manner in which the editor disposes of Rev. Freeborn Garretson. The only grudge that we can imagine the intelligent and talented editor of the *Shield* can owe Rev. Freeborn Garretson is, that that gentleman could not conscientiously hold slaves, and accordingly set them all free, without waiting till they had arrived at the age of 35. He made short work of it. But the reader will say that " W. L. Garrison," and not Rev. Freeborn Garretson, is intended. We reply : That is an implied imputation of ignorance against the able editor of the *Shield*, that we did not wish to make ; and further, that we waited on the

Shield's distinguished editor, and endeavored to enlighten him concerning the historic character of Freeborn Garretson; but no correction appearing in any subsequent issue of that paper, we were left to the presumption that he meant what he said.

This paper is taken by two stewards of Snow Hill Circuit, that refuse to take the *Christian Advocate and Journal*, because it is an abolition incendiary sheet.

Thus matters remained up to the close of the Conference year of 1857.

A few days before the session of the Easton Conference, we met Rev. J. D. Long in the book-room of Higgins and Perkinpine, Philadelphia. Taking us by the hand, and calling the attention of Rev. J. M. McCarter, said : " Allow me to introduce to you —— Junius." The articles of " Junius" were read in the book-room. Comments were made on them; and considerable inquiry instituted to ascertain the author. We will confess to some degree of trepidation when, on the second or third day of the session, no very complimentary allusion was made to " Junius" by a distinguished member of the Conference. We anticipated being called as a witness for the defence in the coming trial of J. D. Long; and consequently our connection with " Junius" would have been fully and publicly known ; and we would have asked a removal from slave territory. But that case not having come before a tribunal, and but little notice having been taken of " Junius," the Elder of the district not being aware of the facts— it was not deemed inadvisable for us to return and finish our term of service on Snow Hill Circuit. It is possible no difficulty *would* have arisen, had it not been that " Mine own familiar friend in whom I trusted, which did eat of my bread," " lifted up his heel against me." On the morning of April 7th, in Salisbury, twenty miles east of Snow Hill, we were informed that there was a tremendous excitement on Snow Hill Circuit in reference to the action of Conference on the " Long," case. We were accused of voting with the majority ; and charged with being the author of " Junius' " letters ; and that the people talked of calling a meeting immediately on our arrival, and sending us away forthwith. Shortly after our arrival in Snow Hill, we stepped into a store occupied by a local preacher and steward. A number of persons being present, a conversation commenced on the exciting topic. A perfect shower of questions was rained down upon us. We stood like the brow of the mountain amid the fury of the tempest. At the commencement of the conversation, two of the stewards entered, and, after adding fresh fury to the agitated elements, they entered a small room, and called in the local preacher and an exhorter. After an interval of a few minutes, we were called into the conclave, and were gravely informed that information had reached them that certain letters had been published in a northern paper ; and from internal evidence, it was presumed that the writer must have been familiar with circumstances that occurred on Snow Hill Circuit. " Did you write them?" We replied : " I have a connection with them." They represented the town to be highly excited, and matters wearing a most serious aspect. I asked for their opinion as to my course of duty. They replied they could not decide until they had seen the letters of "Junius." My situation certainly was not of an agreeable character. We had not a friend with whom to advise ; but frowns, and scoffs, and the cold shoulder met us, even from those whose children, but a few months since, God had made us the instrument of bringing to himself. Aware that explosive elements were around and beneath us, we felt sad and depressed. Sometimes a ray of light would gleam across the dark profound ; again all was darkness. " What should we do ? Will Conference sustain us ? Will conscience ?" It was a dark hour. We were informed that a support could not be had on the circuit. An effort was being made to procure the letters of "Junius." Under these circumstances, glancing over the pages of *Zion's Herald*, we found the following soul-inspiring epistles written to T. J. Quigley, and J. D. Long. These were like light amid darkness—balm to a wounded spirit.

LETTER FROM REV. S. W. COGGESHALL.

NANTUCKET, March 25, 1858.

DEAR BROTHER : The case of Bro. Long, of the Philadelphia Conference, has especially elicited my sympathy. To-day I have written a letter to Dr. Quigley, his prosecutor, as also to two other leading and distinguished members of that old and influential Conference, earnestly praying that the fair fame of our common Methodism might not be tarnished by persistence in the shameful and inquisitorial proceedings in the case of that persecuted brother. I have also written another to Bro. Long himself, inviting him, in case he should be roughly handled by his brethren of the Philadelphia Conference, to attend the approaching sessions of the Providence and New England Conferences, and where, I am sure, that more than a brother's welcome will await him ; and also to bring some of his books with him.

I formed some acquaintance with Bro. Quigley at our late General Conference, of which he was a member, and was led to form a high estimate of his character as a gentleman and a Christian. He is exceedingly mild and gentle in his spirit and manners, so that I was perfectly amazed when I saw his bill of charges against Bro. Long, and which appeared so much unlike the man. But slavery is a fearful thing. One can scarcely come in contact with it without contamination, even if he is a good man. It befouls, begrimes, beslimes and befools all who have to do with it. It communicates a portion of its own character to all who identify themselves with it; and hence, where its interests are concerned, it turns gentlemen into boors, Democrats into despots, and Christians into reprobates.

The brethren of the Philadelphia Conference are a noble, generous body of men, and with good Methodistic instincts. But the whole Peninsula, which is embraced in their territory, is slaveholding, and which identifies them, unfortunately, with this "abomination that maketh desolate." Hence the proposed proceeding in the case of Bro. Long. I enclose you a copy of my letter to Bro. Quigley. I hope that it may be found to express the sentiments of every conservative man in New England; and also, for the reason stated in it, that it may not be esteemed an interference with the concerns of others. In the old New England Conferences, as some of us painfully remember, we suffered members of other Conferences to come in, and *prosecute* our own members, year after year, on counts similar to those now preferred against Bro. Long. Certainly, therefore, to appear in *defence* cannot be considered improper.

Yours, &c.

S. W. COGGESHALL.

NANTUCKET, March 25, 1858.

DEAR BROTHER: You propose to appear before the Philadelphia Conference at its present session as the prosecutor of Bro. J. D. Long, for writing a certain book. This is perfectly inquisitorial—worthy of the middle ages, and of the "mother of harlots." A brother, whose character stands as fair as yours, writes a book on an open question. You reply by an ecclesiastical prosecution, because you suppose that you have a majority to sustain you. It appears to me that it would be much more *manly*, to do as honorable men do, in such cases—answer it by another, if you are *able*; if not, confess the fact. A prosecution in the case is an act of *meanness* and *cowardice*, of which you ought to be most heartily ashamed. Bro. Long's book is on sale at our Book Room—and they don't retail slanders there—and it is before the public; and as for your convincing that public that Bro. Long is guilty of "unchristian conduct," it is simply absurd. If you proceed against him, you will convince them that you are guilty, not only of "unchristian conduct," but also of meanness and of tyranny; and that public, the anti-slavery public, I mean—for it has the most of the presses of the country at its command— will arraign and condemn you. And if you lay the weight of your finger upon Bro. Long, and he appeals, the General Conference will do the same virtually by the reversal of your decision. And this is not all. The matter will go on to the records as a part of the history of the church, and the future historian of the church may handle *your* name as Macaulay now handles the names of certain men of a former age; and I will assure you that a coming generation will not have the fear of the Philadelphia Conference and of the slavebreeders of the Peninsula before their eyes.

Myself and others in the North have been strongly conservative. We have indorsed and defended you; but if you proceed in this matter we can do so no longer. We have been in favor of *tolerating* slavery in the Church as our fathers did, until such times as it can be peacefully disposed of; but if *slavery* does not know its place, but impudently assumes to be *a power* in the Church, it will be tolerated no longer, but will be crushed out; and, I fear, at any cost. As a conservative man, and as one who has indorsed the old-fashioned anti-slavery character of the Border Conferences, I solemnly protest against this proceeding against Bro. Long. The Methodist E. Church is a unit; and we have enough to bear already, on account of the existence of slavery in the Church at all; and to bear the disgrace of the popish and inquisitorial proceeding against Bro. Long is a little too much. We decline it. If the Methodists in the Peninsula don't like the exposure of the abominations of slavery, let them abolish it. That is the only effectual remedy.

I am yours, &c. &c.,

S. W. COGGESHALL.

To Rev. T. J. Quigley, D. D.

At an early day we wrote to the P. E., detailing the circumstances of the case, and concluded thus: "Satisfied my usefulness is at an end on this circuit, I believe it will promote the mutual good of pastor and people for me to be removed." We received a reply and sent the following answer:—

Snow Hill, April 20, 1858.

H. Colclazer—

Rev. and dear Sir: Yours of the 15th was received this morning. I hasten to reply. You say "in relation to your complicity with the ultra-abolitionists of the North." I reply that I have, sir, perhaps as little sympathy with the ultra-abolitionists of the North as yourself. You say "that you regret that you did not at Conference inform me of the fact of your being the author of Junius's letters." I reply, first, that I have told no person that I wrote the letters of Junius, and further, no one has any authority for saying so. 2d. It was my determination to have asked for a removal had any official notice been taken of "Junius;" but little was said, and it was not supposed that I had any hand in the matter. "You would be equally obnoxious on any other circuit within the bounds of Snow Hill District." That is true, and hence the necessity for a removal to one of the upper districts. "Meanwhile, what is to be done for Snow Hill?" I reply that a fair exchange is no robbery, and I am willing to remain until the exchange is made. "Suppose I cannot obtain a place for you, do you intend holding on and take the consequences?" I answer yes, till you remove me. "I will do all I can for you." I am glad to hear you say that. In further reply to your communication, I will say that Junius's letters are now in possession of the stewards of this circuit; they got them a week since. I am inclined to think my letter to you was a little premature. When the stewards came to wait on me with their sage advice and terrible forebodings of the future, my heart felt like a poor little fluttering thing, and I was carried away by the torrent, and for two or three days did not venture from the parsonage; but a number of friends called on me, and I received communications that were as surprising as consoling; and I plucked up courage and ventured abroad, when lo and behold! friends innumerable flocked around me, and assured me of sympathy and support; and I found that the wind did not blow all one way. They contend that I have a right to vote as I please, and write accordingly; and I reply I am willing to stay and *you* take the consequences; I am not afraid but that every church in the *country* will receive me gladly; but at Snow Hill there may be difficulty. I have no fears as to my support. I will not, however, be responsible for consequences. I regret that matters are as they are, and I am willing to do all I can for the sake of peace; I have done nothing wrong, and stand ready to justify myself before the world; I have asked advice of you as my official counsellor; I am willing to submit to the expense and inconvenience of removal, and I rather think it would be better for the circuit for me to remove; but I now submit the whole matter to your discretion. Placing a high estimate on your gentlemanly and Christian character, I remain your humble servant,

J. S. LAME.

I received no further communications from the Presiding Elder, though a number of letters were received by other persons on the circuit, official and unofficial. A steward got one containing this language: "Brother Lame ought to resign. How would Vaughn Smith do? He is a strong man and good preacher. The exhorters and local preachers must take care of the appointments."

A communication was received from Rev. J. M. McCarter, that speaks the nobleness of his nature.

READING, PA., April 8, 1858.

MY DEAR BRO. LAME: Your note surprises me! The people of Snow Hill, Md., certainly can do nothing toward your forcible ejection from among them without committing a great injury upon themselves. You must be a man in your exigency. Trust in God; do nothing rashly, yet be guilty of no act cowardly or inconsistent with truth and right. Make notes of your matters, truthful and without exaggeration; they will be of service in your own defence. I hope the Methodists stand by you—if not, and *you cannot remain* and do your duty as a Methodist preacher, come to Philadelphia. Fear not, if in the line of your duty you have to suffer. Differences of opinion cost something to him who dissents from the current notions of a community.

Very sincerely yours,

REV. J. S. LAME.   J. M. McCARTER.

"A friend in need is a friend, indeed."

The Rev. J. Cunningham was consulted, and most encouraging responses forwarded, as the following extracts show:—

PHILAD., April 23, 1858.

REV. J. S. LAME: Dear Bro. I have just received yours, and I am both *surprised* and *pleased* at what appears to me to be the real state of the case.

The members of the M. E. Church on Snow Hill Circuit, can now prove their loyalty to an anti-slavery church, by sustaining you, or they can prove their pro-slaveryism by refusing to receive and sustain you. I thus advise because, as you say, "the wind does not blow all one way." Preach Jesus Christ and Him crucified with all your power; visit the people pastorally, and if a faithful discharge of your duty does not surround you with friends, then I am mistaken.

I see nothing exceptionable in your reply to Bro. Colclazer. You are conceding too much to a power that seeks to rule, in opposition to all the inherent rights of manhood. If you have done wrong, there is a law, demand to be tried by it. If not, and I believe you have not, stand your ground. I will be glad to hear from you, and also to render you any assistance in my power. I am with you in undying hatred to all oppression.

Yours affectionately,
JAMES CUNNINGHAM.

Knowing the author, in moral prowess, to be a Hercules, the last line of his letter was especially inspiring.

During the week, the most ridiculous stories were put in circulation concerning the case of "Junius;" fabrications that could only have circulation where books and periodicals could not. Southern Senators do not place a very high appreciation on epistolary correspondence, and the circulation of periodicals. Hence, of the nineteen United States Senators who recently voted for increase of postage, seventeen were from the Southern States.

The editor of the *Sunday Dispatch* thinks thus of the lower portion of Delaware. He might have gone nearer the Equator.

The gradual abolition of slavery upon a judicious plan would entitle Delaware to rank among the free States, and encourage an emigration which no slave State can ever experience. Kent and Sussex Counties are in a state of semi-barbarism upon this very account. Thousands of acres lie uncultivated, which, under happier auspices, would be blooming garden spots.

It was an opinion entertained by many friends that the active share we had taken against intemperance in the community, but more particularly in the church, had great influence in the present opposition, and that the devout worshippers of Bacchus seized this juncture as a favorable occasion to fling their barbed and poison-pointed arrows of malignity at the object of their hatred.

The circuit, but more especially the church at Snow Hill, was devastated by the ravages of rum. The terrible torrent was tossing and rolling, and dealing death and damnation from its burning bosom. Brethren of official standing and moneyed influence were concerned not only in its constant use, but its public sale. We determined to lift up our standard, and erect a barrier to impede the progress of that current of "liquid fire and distilled damnation" that was consuming the fair places of our Zion, and leaving naught but wreck and ruin in its trail. For this purpose we designed to preach on the subject, and apply discipline. We opened the temperance battery at a certain appointment, and there certainly was a shaking among the dry bones. The following Sabbath the gospel ordnance was heavily charged, and hot shot fired into the "swellheads," right and left, front and rear. The sanctity of a Christian profession was not allowed to be an impenetrable coat of mail; but arrows of truth from the quiver of the Almighty—gleaming with the lurid light of such sentences as "Wo to him that putteth the bottle to his neighbor's lips!" "And the soul that sinneth, it shall die"—pierced ecclesiastic sinners as well as worldly ones.

During the delivery of the sermon the following passage occurred: "Rum seems to be gifted with the attributes of essentiality and omnipotence. Look abroad: not a project can be conceived but the inspiration must be drawn from the bottle; no enterprise can be attempted and accomplished but by aid of the abominable bottle. Are swine to be butchered; is a building to be reared; a candidate to be elected; a harvest to be reaped; corn to be husked: it must all be done by rum. Men must be purchased and prompted by rum. And even when a venerable, time-honored church-edifice is to be removed—sold by a Methodist, bought by a Methodist, and to be removed by a Methodist—it must be polluted by the rum-bottle. And those sacred walls, that have echoed back the voice of a holy Asbury, and resounded with the sacred songs and fervent prayers of our long-buried fathers and sainted mothers, are to be rendered hideous with the drunken howl and bacchanalian revel of intoxicated negroes. Intoxicating drinks have a remarkably assimilating power; so that the sovereign master, who would scorn to sit at table with a cleanly, sober negro, will drink rum from the same bottle and glass from which the foul and drunken slaves have swilled."

This sermon was thought remarkable for energy of expression and appropriateness of point. And it was generally thought that we were never forgiven for preaching that discourse.

It is, however, due to the piety and good sense of a portion of the community to add that the sermon was highly appreciated by some, and encouraging testimonials were received of its benevolent effects.

On Sabbath morning, April 25, we preached in Snow Hill. The audience was quite diminutive. *One* active official member was in attendance, but not a single member of the ecclesiastical liquor-loving fraternity was present. The leader of the choir, tried and true, was in his seat; and though the *members* of the choir had remained at home, or gone elsewhere to tune their joyful songs, yet, the congregation joining in the song with a familiar tune, the volumes of praise swept up to the ear of the Lord God of Sabaoth. The singing may not have been so artistic in its execution, but was more inspiring in its effects.

During the evening service we had the same select auditory. What we lacked in quantity was fully supplied in quality, for not a rumsucker, rumseller, or follower of Pharaoh was present. On the following day those who had the awful temerity to give audience to the ministrations of the "white nigger"—as "Junius" was termed— were called on to endure a terrible lingual castigation. "Such conduct was perfectly disgraceful and disorganizing." "Besides, it is bidding God-speed to a liar and a hypocrite." The reply of one was, "I am a Lame man from the crown of my head to the sole of my foot."

Saturday evening, May 8th, the Presiding Elder arrived at the house of a steward in Snow Hill. The Sabbath following was the day of our quarterly meeting. The place of holding the meeting was five miles from the town of Snow Hill. His appointments were for Sabbath night and Monday morning; but, contrary to all precedent except his own, he preached in Snow Hill on Sabbath morning. That his effort was appreciated, the following that appeared in the next issue of the town paper, will testify :—

REV. HENRY COLCLAZER.

This gentleman preached in the Methodist Episcopal Church, in Snow Hill, on Sunday the 9th inst. Although his visit was somewhat unexpected, and the notice of his intention to preach given but an hour before service, yet his high reputation for pulpit eloquence obtained for him a very large congregation. We have seldom heard a more powerful sermon. One of the most prominent characteristics of his preaching is, that it goes right to the mark, and with unspeakable distinctness, says to the conscience of each individual— "Thou art the man."

The reader may inquire how it happened that "notice of his intention to preach was not given till an hour before service." He arrived in Snow Hill about dusk on Saturday; and yet there was "no notice of his intention to preach but an hour before service !" Perhaps the disclosures of one well calculated to testify in the case may throw some light on this extraordinary proceeding. According to that testimony, he was waited on by certain parties from the hour of his arrival, until a late moment on Saturday night ; and that he was beleaguered early on Sabbath morning. That most terrible representations were made to the Elder, his own declarations to the writer are ample evidence. At night the country appointment was favored with an excellent sermon from his Eldership. We retired from the church to room together during the night. As the moments passed away till the hour of 12, we were entertained with cigar smoke, and a most dolorous account of our imbroglio. He was fearful that the letters of " Junius" (unfortunate I call them) would be published in the *Shield*, and that incendiary remarks, added by the editor, would excite the populace to deeds of desperation. He was fearful that we were not aware of the extent and violence of the opposition ; that the matter had become so complicated that certain parties would demand an explanation at all hazards. He had been trying to make an exchange, but had failed ; that if we were out of the way he could supply our place.

Monday morning arrived. The P. E. preached a fine sermon, during the delivery of which the Discipline of the M. E. Church was lauded and magnified, and eulogized as a monument of wisdom ; even the term "sublime" was applied to it. Immediately after service the Quarterly Conference opened. The opposition had arrived in full force, and, as if anticipating a long pull, a strong pull, and a pull altogether, had brought provisions for man and beast. But the friends of " Junius," presuming that the matter would be speedily and satisfactorily settled—relying on the Christian forbearance of the opposition—expected to reach home by one o'clock P. M. The Rev. Secretary of the Conference being so much interested, and becoming a *particeps criminis*, kept no notes of the Conference. But the minutes were written out by the author next day, and subsequently submitted to a meeting composed of those who were at the Conference ; and the united verdict was given in favor of their fidelity. An opinion was expressed that the malignity and devilish daring of the opposition were but partially revealed in this record. We here present a record of the proceedings :—

MINUTES OF THE QUARTERLY CONFERENCE.

MONDAY, May 10, 1858.

At 12 M. the Quarterly Conference opened—all the members of our Board of Stewards slaveholders. The Board was not full; and as there was but one member for the three churches east of the river, and as three members were from Snow Hill charge, I nominated a brother. Objections were offered, not to the man, but to the nomination. A steward asked why it was desired to fill the board at this meeting—why not wait? I replied that "I made the same nomination three months since; but the man, who now objected to confirm this nomination, then said that, inasmuch as a steward had been removed because he had been selling rum, it was probable that he would soon quit the business, and that it might be well to readmit him at the next Quarterly Meeting. So now the next Quarterly Meeting has arrived, I now nominate another brother." It was then mentioned that this brother was not eligible. "No," another remarked, "he is not *legible!* for he has not been a member of church a year." The Elder so ruled. It was also said that Spring Hill was more entitled to a steward than Furnace appointment. I then arose and nominated a worthy brother from Spring Hill. A brother then thought it was inexpedient at this period to have another steward. The same brother stated that the board only lacked one of being full, as the disciplinary number was from 5 to 7. The Elder so ruled. The vote on the confirmation of the nomination was taken; it was pronounced lost; I called for a division, and the vote stood 8 to 7; it was carried. But something was said about some brother voting misunderstandingly; so the vote was taken over again, and that time there was a tie; and, for want of a majority, the Elder decided it lost.

The next business was making the apportionment for next year. How much should it be? A motion was made that it should continue the same as last year. —— thought it could not be raised, if the money collected this morning is a criterion, as it was exceedingly small. I replied that it was no criterion, as the time of the Quarterly Meeting was not known till the Saturday before its commencement; that at some appointments it was not known at all, in which case it had to be informally announced at the church at which it was held; and that at the first Quarterly Meeting for 1857, I received the munificent sum of $16.00, and my colleague $12.00; and that the appropriation of last year had not been paid. Brother Turpin replied that it should be, as far as he was concerned. A steward said that he had tried as usual, and *one* man had refused to give. Dr. Jones said that he mentioned the matter to the leaders, and that the sum of $1.60 had been received; and that he represented a charge that paid last year nearly $100, but that this year he did not think that one-fifth of that amount could be realized. Brothers Lacompt and Powell made statements of a similar character. The latter stated that some of his class were offended when he asked for quarterage. Then I arose, and remarked: "Like people, like priest; it was to be expected that the people would think and act as their leaders; that neither of these brethren came to hear me preach; that they had stood aloof from me; but that a number of their class were my friends, and would gladly pay. But that these brethren, having taken a stand against me, had influenced the class." The Elder told me I must cease speaking, as I was offensively personal. I stopped. The brethren stated that they did wait on their classes. At this juncture, Brother Powell arose and said that the true question was:

Can we sustain Brother Lame? I added: "That is the true question; why not meet it like men?"

Dr. Jones arose, and gave as his judgment that J. S. Lame could not be sustained. Such was the opinion of Brothers Turpin, Powell, and Lacompt. Brother Wm. K. Rowley stated that Spring Hill stood as she ever had stood —warm friends of Brother Lame. Brother George Hudson said the same of Furnace and Holland's. I stated that I would take the responsibility of a support. The question then occurred on the motion for the amount to be the same as last year. The question was put and carried in the affirmative. Dr. Jones said that a brother had not voted understandingly. The brother replied that he did; he voted to give our preacher the same as he had last year; that if he were to stay among us, he did not wish him to be turned out upon the barrens. Brother Turpin asked whether the Board of Stewards were responsible. The Elder replied that they were not responsible in the sense of a legal contract; but that as a committee of ways and means, they were expected to use their efforts and influence to raise the amount. Brother Turpin then offered his resignation, followed by the whole Board. The Elder then reiterated his remarks about the responsibility. A brother still pressed his resignation; the question was put and not accepted.

I then arose and stated that I did not wish to be considered rebellious. Let the Board of Stewards, as my official advisers, I said, draw up an instrument, signed by a majority of the Board, advising me to retire; and that I would take that as the voice of the church; or, if a majority of the Quarterly Conference would advise my withdrawal; or, if the Elder would dismiss me; or, if he will make an exchange, that I would be satisfied. I added that I did not wish to be driven away, but wished them to give me their written opinion that I ought to retire, and that the good of the Circuit demanded it, and that I did not feel myself free to cut loose from all connection from any field of labor; I thought that by that act I located myself; and that at Conference I must give a satisfactory reason why I abandoned my work. And what, I asked, could I say? I could not say that a majority asked for my removal; I could not say that I was afraid that I would not get a support. What self-defence could I make before Conference? I could simply say that a faction at Snow Hill desired me to leave, and that I got scared and ran off; I was waxing warm, and said that if the gray hairs of the venerable David Daily could not protect him from insult, how was it expected that—At this point the Elder interposed, and asked whether it was not possible to make a compromise; perhaps, he thought, I might express regret for the past, and give a pledge for the future; he merely suggested it; said it was no use to do all talking; that we were getting twisted.

The Elder suggested the propriety of the stewards retiring to see if they could agree upon any plan; they retired; in about ten minutes they returned; said that they had determined not to give me the recommendation that I asked for; that I was the author of the disturbance, and that I must bear the responsibility. I arose and replied that I was perfectly satisfied, delighted to bear all responsibility; that I did not fear the financial results. The Elder said that I did not seem to feel the difficulty. I replied that I did feel and appreciate the difficulty; but why, I asked, did not the stewards advise me in regard to the matter? The Elder said that he had seen and felt this difficulty ever since the commencement; that it had cost him much trouble; that he had written to the Presiding Elders of the upper districts to see if an exchange could be made; that he had been referred to a brother through Bro. Combe.

Some of the members of the opposition said that they would refer the matter to him. He then said that if they referred the matter to him, he would decide at once that the exchange would not do. He said that he might exercise arbitrary powers and cut Bro. Lame loose, but he did not think the Discipline vested in him that prerogative. Bro. —— said that he had been thinking he ought not to hear Bro. Lame preach, and receive the sacrament from his hands. Bro. —— said that the reason that *he* did not hear him preach was that he understood he thought that all that came to hear him preach indorsed his course. I said I wished to know whether I had done anything that the Discipline condemns. "A few days since," I continued, "a brother now on this floor asked a certain brother if charges were to be preferred against Bro. Lame at the quarterly meeting. He replied no; he had done nothing that the Discipline condemns. It will bear him out in all that he has done, and there is our difficulty. And there is the man that said it," pointing to Bro. ——. He said not a word.

I was then interrupted by the Presiding Elder. A call was then made for the letters of "Junius." I raised the question how that was to affect my case, as I had never confessed myself the author of "Junius's" letters. S. T—— arose and gave an account of the first informal meeting of the stewards, in which, he said, I stated that I had confessed a guilty connection with them, and that I affirmed that they would not approve of them; that I had been writing what by my own acknowledgment they would not approve. I replied that my meaning in using the words "a guilty connection" was, that if any guilt at all attached, I was guilty; and that my meaning in saying that they would not be approved was that they, the stewards, and all like them, would not approve them, for at that very interview Bros. —— and —— said that they would not take the *Christian Advocate* because it was an abolition sheet; consequently they would not approve "Junius." I protested against the reading of the letters of "Junius." As I did not state my connection with them, it was asked, "Do they contain your sentiments? do you indorse them?" I replied, "I do. They are an indorsement and defence of J. D. Long's book." "Mr. Elder," it was asked, "what is your opinion of J. D. Long's book?" "Oh, as for my opinion, I deem it beneath contempt." I was asked, "What is the extent of your connection with 'Junius'?" The Elder pressed the question. "Now, Lame, like an honest fellow, acknowledge that you are the author. Be candid." I replied, "I neither affirm nor deny." "Well," rejoined the Elder, "you furnished the facts, and McCarter put them in shape." I replied, "You have no authority to say that; I neither affirm nor deny." Bro. —— then said that it was easy to locate the facts narrated in "Junius's" letters, and that they contained misstatements.

They were ordered to be read. Dr. Jones was asked to read them; he demurred, and asked Bro. Colclazer to do so, who declined. I then offered to read them. Dr. Jones, stating that he did not wish the brethren to think he did it through improper feelings, then read "Junius." During the reading he so mumbled his words as to make it difficult for the hearer to separate the quotations from Long from the language of "Junius." As the reader came to the point where fourteen slaves are stated to have absconded from the steward of a certain circuit, the Elder said, "That is Bro. P——. He is a very fine man and a kind master." When the reading was concluded, a brother arose and announced that he must now change his vote. (The reason why, I have since heard.) Bro. Lacompt then arose and commented at considerable length on the articles, particularly on certain supposed cases. He was not interrupted. I then arose to reply, and was proceeding to say that, after such a terrible onslaught, I hardly recognized my own moral identity, when I received a severe rebuke from the Presiding Elder for my levity, and for not feeling the difficulty that the circuit was in. I retorted that I did feel the difficulty, and was willing to use all honorable means for its removal; and further stated that the stewards either did not tell the truth, or else I was compelled to charge cowardice upon them. Here I was interrupted by the Presiding Elder again. I then continued: "for the Board of Stewards charge me with being an abolitionist—a misrepresenter; they affirm that distraction, division, and appalling calamities will follow; and now, in view of all these evils, they refuse to simply say, officially, that, for the good of the circuit, I ought to leave. Now, they do not believe what they say, or they must be cowards." Here I was interrupted again. I had a vast amount of rebutting evidence, and what, in my judgment, was amply sufficient to overthrow the speech of ——.

A proposition was made to make no appropriation for the support of the ministry on Snow Hill Circuit. I arose and announced how the passage of that resolution would be received. It, however, passed.

I then commenced making some pertinent remarks, and designed to review the whole question, but was again insulted and silenced by the Elder—not having been permitted on one occasion to express my thoughts without interruption. My feelings became aroused. Four mortal hours I had stood the contest; and deeming the course of the Presiding Elder partial, unwise, and unjust, firmly believing that it was impossible for me to get justice, I arose, took my hat and coat, and said: "I see it is impossible for me to get justice here. I appeal from you to the world." I left the house, followed by a number of my friends. I got on my horse; got off again, and scraped the dust from my feet against my persecutors.

The Elder received all the money paid to the Appropriating Committee, so that from the stewards I have not received a single cent. During the proceeding the President remarked that if I were out of the way he could supply my place.

The above, I believe, is a faithful record of the proceedings of the first Quarterly Meeting Conference for Snow Hill Circuit, held in Furnace Church, May 10, 1858.

J. S. LAME.

The people in the South have a most happy faculty of mingling opposites, and piously serving the Devil. A brother in the Conference, while making a special plea for my condemnation, spoke of the lofty motives by which he was moved, and how he desired to promote God's glory; and while he contemplated his more than seraphic devotion, he burst into tears. Quite a piece with the Southern Commercial Convention, recently in session, that opened its meeting with prayer, and then debated a resolution favoring the opening of the slave-trade.

We understood the reason why the Board of Stewards refused the document we desired was, that they were fearful it would be given

49

to the press ; but were bent on ignominiously expelling me from the Circuit. So they determined to propose and pass the starvation resolution.

The minutes state that, after the reading of " Junius," one member changed his vote. The reason suggested to us was this : In one of the epistles of " Junius," a Methodist master is spoken of who " boasted of the thorough and efficacious cowhiding he had administered to his slave women." This good brother, who changed his vote, it seems on one occasion, becoming provoked at the misconduct of one of his colored women, beat and stamped her to that degree, that medical aid was requisite to preserve life and restore health. It seems that the flagellation of females is of frequent occurrence on the Eastern Shore ; for another brother stoutly maintained that " Junius" meant him, for it was his case described. We learned that this brother employed a broom-handle for a rod of correction. And still another brother complained that " Junius" had given to the public the fact that he had cudgelled his black women ; but gave the assurance that the whipping was deserved. Now we have to tell all these dear brethren, " Junius" meant neither. It was a Methodist in another county to which he alluded.

The Quarterly Conference would not allow us a single foot of honorable ground upon which to stand ; but seemed to have assembled with the pre-determination to crush us out. But we certainly had reason for admiring their forbearance, for, on arriving at home, we were told that an ex-member of the Quarterly Conference had determined to head a mob, and, after treating us to a mess of ancient odorous eggs, disgracefully drive us off. We returned an indignant reply to the message, and determined that " live or die, survive or perish, sink or swim," we would not desert our post till our judgment was convinced that we ought to leave.

After much prayer, and mature deliberation on the following points, we concluded to make a peace-offering of ourself.

1st. The Quarterly Conference—the highest tribunal on the Circuit —had determined to give us no support; every member of the Board of Stewards was a slaveholder, and sanguinarily opposed us ; money paid into the hand of the Stewards to be handed us we never got.

2d. But a tithe of the members and congregation of Snow Hill would hear us preach.

3d. We had been notified that we might expect personal violence.

4

Though we might be willing, personally, to offer our life as a sacrifice, we had a wife and boy, whose lives we did not feel free to involve.

4th. Spies were continually maintaining watch over our words and acts—even daring to enter our family circle to engender discord, and to filch facts or falsehoods through the simplicity of a domestic.

5th. A threat was made that the parsonage should be burned.

6th. We were influenced by the advice of one who, on this subject, ought to be a competent guide : "I advise you to leave ; 1st. They will starve you out ; or, 2dly, they will do you some personal violence, for slavery is as cruel as the grave ; or 3dly, they will get up some disgraceful charge against you. My interest in you induces me to admonish you to leave immediately." (J. D. LONG.)

7th. The command of Christ, "When they persecute you in this city, flee ye into another."

8th. And last, though not least, we trusted that this course would soften the asperity of feeling, and heal the unhappy divisions existing on the Circuit.

Accordingly, we retired.

Zion's Herald's able editor thought us lucky, as we saw this paragraph in the next issue of that valuable journal.

JUNIUS.

We understand that a member of the Philadelphia Conference, suspected of being the author of the letters in *Zion's Herald*, signed "Junius," has been driven on account of that suspicion from Maryland, and forced to flee to free soil. He has now taken refuge in Philadelphia, and we shall be able soon to lay before our readers a fuller account of his expatriation. This is a free land, and the man supposed to be guilty of writing those letters in *Zion's Herald* may consider himself lucky that he was not sent at once to heaven from the lowest limb of the nearest tree.

From the action of the Conference we supposed ourself *expelled* from the Circuit ; but the *Shield* seemed to think otherwise, as that Illuminator contained this notice in the first number following the quarterly meeting :—

RESIGNATION.

Rev. J. S. Lame, who was appointed Senior Clergyman on Snow Hill Circuit, at the late session of the Philadelphia Annual Conference, resigned his charge, at the Quarterly Conference held at the Furnace Church, on Monday the 10th inst. Rev. Vaughan Smith is expected to assume his place.

Which we replied to as follows :—

CORRECTION.

MR. EDITOR :—The paragraph under the caption of "Resignation," in your last issue, is incorrect, no such resignation having taken place. The fact of the case is simply this: A motion was made in the Conference, that no appropriation be made in this quarter, for the support of the ministry on Snow Hill Circuit. It was distinctly announced that should the motion carry, it would be considered equivalent to a vote of dismissal; the motion (we believe) prevailed.

J. S. LAME.

Considering that we were divorced from our field of labor, we made preparations to leave, disposing of our riding establishment at considerable sacrifice.

A rumor having got in circulation that the deficiency in the salary of last year, and that the first quarter of the present year were to be paid, we stated that we feared that the report was a *ruse* to prevent our friends from tendering material aid, and so it proved. Thus the sacred, repeated, and public promises of the Stewards were violated; and we were crushed out and driven off without a single dollar of remuneration. But, on the afternoon of our departure, we were stopped in the street by a merchant steward, and a note or money demanded for a small debt. We were not, however, without friends. There are as noble hearts on that field of labor as ever beat in mortal bosom. Men, and women too, there dared to stem the torrent that had set against us, and sympathized with and succored their friend in the hour of extremity. Noble spirits, self-sacrificing in devotion, and uniting in toil. It would afford much pleasure to mention their names, did not such mention expose them to the same fiery trial that has tried us. May the best blessings of God be their everlasting inheritance! Amen.

The succeeding Sabbath, by invitation, we preached at Spring Hill. During the sermon the lamentations of the congregation were overwhelming. They presented us with a purse of $50. Let not the antislavery men of the North presume that there are no righteous men in Sodom. There are some who walk amid rum and slavery's pollutions with their white garments unspotted, and who bear their testimony against the sum of all villanies; but they are brow-beaten and borne down by their ecclesiastic and political lords and masters. They will yet be heard, and more terrible will be the explosion from the long repression. The good seed has been sown—the leaven is working in the mass, political and ecclesiastic. Let not the Extirpationists abate one jot of heart or effort, and freedom yet shall triumph.

A portion of the people, writhing under a poignant sense of the scandalous outrage committed against the dignity of the Circuit, called an indignation meeting, and passed the subjoined resolutions :—

Joint Meeting of the Members of Holland's and Furnace, held at Furnace Chapel this 22d day of May, 1858.

The meeting was opened by prayer, after which —— was called to the Chair, and —— elected Secretary.

The following preamble and resolutions were unanimously adopted :—

Whereas, The Board of Stewards, of Snow Hill Circuit, and principal men of Snow Hill appointment, having in our opinion proved disloyal to the Philadelphia Annual Conference in rejecting the minister thereby sent, by refusing at the late Quarterly Conference of said Circuit, to give said minister a support, and by other unwise and unjust treatment unto him :

We, the members of the classes at Holland's and Furnace appointments, desiring to remain loyal to the aforesaid Annual Conference, and being unwilling to coincide with the above said Stewards and principal men, or in anywise to sanction their course, do offer and make the following resolutions, being determined to abide thereby ; and we do cordially invite any and all appointments of like sentiments to unite with us in endeavoring to preserve and perpetuate the peace, purity, and general good of the M. E. Church in our midst.

1st. Resolved, That we retain our connection with the Philadelphia Annual Conference.

2d. Resolved, That we can no longer hold connection or affiliation with Snow Hill appointment.

3d. Resolved, That we pay nothing to the support of any minister sent to Snow Hill Circuit, so long as we are connected with Snow Hill appointment.

4th. Resolved, We knowing the sentiments of our Spring Hill and Connor's brethren, do invite them to join us in petitioning the Presiding Elder to send us a single minister on our own account.

5th. Resolved, That we send a committee to wait on the two-above-named appointments, asking their co-operation.

——, ——, —— were elected to lay the proceedings of this meeting before our Spring Hill and Connor's brethren, asking their co-operation.

After which the meeting adjourned.

Not being able to dispose of our property as soon as the Arabs desired, we received a kindly notice that, if we were not gone by a certain day, the house would be pulled down over our head.

Since our departure from the Circuit, we have received a number of letters that fully illustrate and confirm the account herein given, and the opinion we have formed of the ruling spirits on Snow Hill Circuit.

SNOW HILL, June 8, 1858.

DEAR BROTHER LAME : You may know that we were all glad to hear from you, and to know that you had got out from among your persecutors ; yet I believe you have as many friends down here as you have enemies. We are getting no better very fast; that is, this disturbance I mean. Mr. Smith preached at the Furnace last Sunday, and he had four of the class to hear him; and they went to let him know how we stood.

We still have our prayer meetings, and there are not many petitions sent up to heaven but what our absent pastor is thought of. May heaven's richest blessings be poured down on yourself and family wherever you may go.

We all send our love to you and family. We are as well as common, and —— is hard down on that clique as ever.

And another speaks plainly, thus:—

SNOW HILL, June 11th, 1858.

MY VERY DEAR BROTHER: Yours came to hand on the 6th inst., and I was very glad to find that you had safely arrived among your friends, for of all places in this world of ours home and friends must be the most desirable to the oppressed and persecuted. The Snow Hill Inquisition seem determined to drive us into measures. They have employed the Rev. Vaughan Smith, as I understand, and say we must help to support him. He preached at Holland and Furnace on last Sabbath, to not an overly-crowded congregation. At Holland there were about 15 persons out, but not a single member of the class; no one to invite them to dine. As it happened there was a good radical out, who took them home with him and fed them, as I suppose. At the Furnace there was about the same turn out, except there was four of our members out, two of whom were sent to read our resolutions to him. I forgot to state that Brother ——, our Girard of Snow Hill, and ——, went with Brother Smith as his body guards, I suppose lest we upstarts, mushrooms, abolitionists, rebels, and foresters, should mob him. One good brother remarked that he thought in all probability if their carriage had been searched a bottle of brandy or rot-gut whiskey would have been found. I think that the brother was very pious when he made that remark; don't you? Brother Smith says he is going to preach for us till the quarterly meeting; he says we have rebelled. Be that as it may, I expect he will find more rebellion at his next appointment at the aforesaid places.

Pretty highhanded business, I think, when a few rich whiskey-drinking members of Snow Hill shall say who shall preach and who shall not preach; and who shall be supported and who driven away. The battle is just as warm now as when you left, and I am determined to fight as long as there is one left. Pray for us, we need your prayers.

You said you were under so many obligations to me for my kindness to you. Now I don't want to hear that any more. I did nothing more than my duty, for I never shall be able to satisfy the debt of gratitude I owe to you, and God alone can reward you for what you have done for me. God bless you, Brother Lame. I expect to meet you in that Bright World where there are no farewells given; and if I am never permitted to see you again in this world, go on, I'll meet you in Heaven by the grace of God. The madame joins me in love to you and yours. I shall write again whenever anything transpires worthy of note. God bless you: good-bye.

Your brother in Christ,

—— ——.

Please write me again soon.

And still another letter:—

DEAR BRO. LAME: Your letter came to hand. We are glad to hear you are all well. We at present are like sheep without a shepherd, though I believe the stewards are about to force upon us a man of their choice. The Saturday after you left they met Mr. Smith, and authorized him to preach all around the circuit. The next day (Sabbath) he preached in Snow Hill, much to their satisfaction. Yesterday he went to Holland's in the morning; found a few persons there, but none of the principal members; there being no Methodist there to invite them to dinner. He (Mr. Smith) let them know we had no right to separate ourselves from the circuit, and that he should preach there until the Quarterly Meeting.

Dear Brother, my heart is sick when I think of the devastation and ruin those men have brought upon the Church. She is rent in pieces, and, although some of them have acknowledged themselves in the wrong, they still persist in the wrong; those very men who professed in Conference to be aiming at the glory of God and good of the Church. Actions speak louder than words, and their acts most certainly contradict their words. The meanest, lowest, and most unlikely falsehoods are being circulated about yourself. I am so mortified at the conduct of the stewards I feel ashamed to walk the public streets. The truly respectable men in the community unite in crying shame upon them. I do not feel hatred or malice toward those men; but I feel grieved at their conduct, and over the ruin of the Church. It will take years to obliterate the disgrace which has been inflicted upon her.

Last night we had prayer meeting at Mr. ——; had a good time.

You know, Bro. Lame, that we have not rebelled against the government of the Church, but have refused to unite with the rebellious party, and will not be governed by that faction of which we consider the Elder a member.

—— —— is going to make out the proceedings of the Quarterly Conference, and publish it in the *Shield*. You know what it will be without my telling you—a mass of falsehoods. The class send their love to you and yours.

Your humble friend,

—— ——.

And the following will demonstrate that we have not spoken too harshly of that miserable clique at Snow Hill:—

SNOW HILL, August 5, 1858.

DEAR BROTHER LAME: I suppose this letter is somewhat unexpected to you, but I had intended to write to you a good while ago, and I have at last got at it; but I am poorly prepared to think or write on any subject to-day, for my nerves are completely unstrung; so when you read this take off your ministerial glasses and put on your corn-field ones, if you have any.

Well, Brother Lame, the great battle is fought and the victory won; but old Furnace still stands unharmed, still wearing her armor in defiance of oppression and the scoffs of our tyrannical lawgivers. Since you left us we have had a double share of the Gospel, although one-half of it, judging from the attendance, seemed not to be *good news*. Messrs. Newman and Miller have been our preachers. Messrs. Smith and Atkins of course came from Rome, and preached according to her authority, for one quarter, for the sum of 000—I mean from Holland's and Furnace. Oh, what rebels these two appointments are.

No wonder the hard times affect them (?) We waited on the Rev. Vaughan Smith. His first appointment at the Furnace showed him the proceedings of our meeting (of which you know all about); he immediately branded us rebels and revolutionizers. When he said that we came very near exploding; but just at that moment some one politely intimated that it was time to preach, so Brother Smith went in and told us to "humble *ourselves* under the mighty hand of God, and in due time *we should* be exalted."

Smith and Atkins, Newman and Miller have preached alternately every Sabbath, last Sabbath excepted, which was Quarterly at Spring Hill and Horntown. The Quarterly Meeting Conference was held Saturday. Rev. Mr. Colclazer presided; ex-presiding Elder and Bishop —— present. Soon as G—— introduced his little matter, Mr. Colclazer could not refrain a very contemptuous laugh, asking him to do what was already done; but G——, nothing daunted, pressed his suit, and finally succeeded. Mr. Smith seemed disposed never to give us up.

G—— told the Elder he might do just as he pleased about it, as that was the last appeal that would ever be made to him or any one else on the subject; that we had determined to go to Newtown Circuit and carry the house with us, there being a *fortunate* mistake in the deed. O! gracious, what a mad set of folks there was there; but at last it got before the Conference, and was carried by a unanimous vote. Now we've bid them a long good-bye. On Monday G—— went to the Newtown Quarterly Meeting, held at Swan's Gut. That Conference received Holland's and Furnace appointments as a part of Newtown Circuit.

Brother Newman has been a strong friend to us. He defends us whenever we are attacked. I forgot to tell you he was at the Spring Hill Quarterly Conference, but of course had no voice, unless personally assailed, which was frequently done during Conference; but he as often met and refuted them. He was charged with being the originator of the *great rebellion*, and a defender of revolutionizers. And now we are at last free from our oppressors, although we have gone with the anathemas of Snow Hill officials, Presiding Elder, too, upon our guilty heads!

Now, if Snow Hill will let us alone, we will let them alone; but it seems to be an impossibility for them to quit talking on the subject. Mr. ——, I am told, has left the Church. Poor man! I pity him; he has to bear a great deal from ——; he watches him day and night, and tries to twist everything he says into a ——.

I am told Spring Hill is very much dissatisfied because she did not get off with us. Wesleyville is also dissatisfied.

I am told Snow Hill wants to send Atkins home, and Newark protests it shall not be done. Rev. Mr. Smith says so; —— says that the Board of Stewards on Snow Hill Circuit is not worth powder enough to blow them to the ——. We are getting along first rate at the Furnace.

Family join me in love to Mrs. Lame and yourself. Good-bye.

I remain your unworthy friend,

—— ——.

Let me assure the Northern Extirpationists that though he may be the object of many a fool-born jest—though he may be despised and derided, yet there are ebony lips that hourly pronounce benedictions on his head, and waft prayers to high Heaven for the time of the unrequited toil to terminate. These people well understood the cause of their pastor's expulsion. Many were the happy hours we had together; we have preached to them, when our voice would be lost in a gust of praise—we had led them in class, and acted as their protector, and baptized their little ones, and married their youth. During the fortnight immediately preceding our departure, we baptized some thirty little ones. Many were the stolen visits of these poor blacks to the parsonage with tear-gemmed eye, and a new quarter dollar in their hand; they invoked showers of blessings upon us; they sympathized in our sorrows and talked of that better and brighter land where partings are forever unknown. We told them frankly the real cause of our expulsion. "Ah, yes, de preacher dat likes us, de white folks neber likes." The last night of our stay in Rome, two colored couple came to be married, accompanied by friends innumerable. They made up a sum of money as a testimonial of their gratitude; and, on the morning of our departure, as the boat pushed off, one ran up to the wharf, thrust his hands into his pocket, brought up a quarter, flung it on the deck of the moving boat, and cried, " Good-bye—meet you up dar," energetically pointing skyward. The friendship of our white friends continued to the last; and like Paul they accompanied us to the boat; sorrowing most of all for the words that were spoken that they should see our face no more; and we took our everlasting flight from Maryland—the land of the free—the home of the brave—and the asylum of the oppressed !

And now we will ask the reader to suffer a word. The above, we believe, is a plain impassioned statement of facts. Many more facts might have been added, and those we have given might have been highly colored; but we think we have avoided all strong and exciting expressions. We have seen sights, and heard sounds, that might make the cheeks of a devil blush for his honor. We have seen the child of three summers torn from its mother's convulsive grasp where her groans might almost be heard by the minister in the M. E. Sanctuary. We have seen the panting fugitive dragged back to his hated task. We have seen the ministers of Christ offer their reward for the return of his runaways; and we have known one to spend the sacred Sabbath in getting the dogs of the law to fasten their fangs in the flesh of his brother—(one of his own color). We have seen the wife violently separated from the husband; and the children separated from the mother.

These are the natural and inevitable product of the system of slavery—a system that finds a thousand apologists. Learned Doctors of Divinity will tell us that this monster should still be spared in the church, be baptized at the altar of our holy Christianity, and be christened a divine institution. There is not a more successful way to people the dominions of the damned with the slaves of the South than the publication of a doctrine like this; it is stench in their nostrils, and an abomination to their moral sense. And the minister of Christ talks the miserable twaddle about "cursed be Canaan;" and tells us that Divine Providence brought the heathen African to America to be christianized; reminding us of a comment made on this new revelation: that "God must have been hard up for a plan to convert heathens." This proposition is too glaringly absurd, and shockingly blasphemous, for further comment. If this be theology, from theology, good Lord, deliver us! We will take the Bible without note or comment, and if this be reason, let us be guided by the instinct of nature. But we have recently been lectured on the awful temerity of a young man assuming our position. We have been told that days should speak, and multitude of years should teach wisdom. Our only apology for being young—is that God has not yet made us any older. But we are almost as old as he who said to his countrymen, "Ye serpents, ye generation of vipers, how can ye escape the damnation of hell?"

Some would-be leaders discourse to us on the manifest impropriety of opposing the connection of good men with the institution, as they are without controversy the mildest masters; and to cut off, they say, the possibility of the slave being connected with a Christian master is but to aggravate the evils of his bondage. This reasoning finds its parallel in the following: Piracy is a bad practice; but its horrors are aggravated by the men engaged in it; *therefore*, good men—Methodists—should be allowed to be pirates, to mitigate the miseries of piracy. Again: Rum-selling is an unfortunate business, but its evils are greatly aggravated by the class of men who engage in it; *ergo*, good men—Methodists—should be allowed to be rumsellers, for they may modify its shocking evils. "Come out from among them, and be ye separate, saith the Lord, and touch not the unclean thing; and I will receive you." Slavery founded on manstealing is a moral evil. But American slavery is founded on manstealing. The major proposition will be admitted as correct; the minor, we think, must be admitted as historic truth; therefore, the conclusion is irresistible, that American slavery is a moral evil. Now the Apostle exhorts us to shun the very appearance of evil.

Let the statesman glance over our magnificent territorial domain, sweeping from the shores of the Atlantic on the east to the waves of the Pacific on the west, adorned with mountain, lake, and river—a land bought by the bravery, and consecrated by the blood, of our forefathers—a land which, though the fairest beneath the sun, is prostituted to tyranny more galling than Great Britain *ever* imposed—a land where pæans to liberty mingle with the groans of the oppressed and the howl of the slave; a land of law, and yet where millions are outlawed without any crime, but that of color; a country whose fundamental principle is, that " all men are born free and equal," while it embraces in her bosom millions of men reduced to chattels. Let the statesman read, reflect, and act.

Let the Christian philanthropist survey the scene. A Howard penetrated the prisons of Europe to mitigate suffering and preach deliverance to the captive. The Southern part of our Union is one vast penitentiary, where multitudes are incarcerated in hopeless fetters. It boasts of its Bibles, and yet its laws and its customs deny to myriads the power to acquire a proper knowledge of the Bible. It claims to be a land of intelligence, while it permits multitudes to remain in sottish ignorance; a land of missionaries, while millions of heathens of all colors are in its midst. Eyes long used to weeping are turned towards the North, as the land of promise; hearts long crushed with a weight of woe are uttering deep groans for deliverance. Ethiopia in America is stretching out her hands. Shall she call in vain? Will none hear her impassioned appeal? The hard-handed, back-bowed son of unrequited toil, sweating out fortunes for his remorseless master, cries for mercy. The young man of talent, that feels the first throbbing of a noble nature, yearning to live to bless and benefit mankind in a sphere of freedom, asks your help. That youth—through whose veins flows a large preponderance of Anglo-Saxon blood—more keenly feels the deep degradation that his white brother imposes upon him, and in the indignant outburst of his feelings exclaims : " My punishment is greater than I can bear. Who shall deliver me from the body of this death?" The mother, the panting, unpitied mother, as she convulsively clings to the child of her affections, and as half damned man rudely and ruthlessly wrenches it from her bosom, falls fainting to the earth, and, as she returns to consciousness, sends up her first long loud wail.

Let her piercing appeal penetrate your heart, and arouse your slumbering energies. Let these united appeals, like the combined tones of a thousand thunders, awake the dreaming church.

Minister of Christ, idolatry was a political institution, and the bread and butter of multitudes depended on its revenues; and yet Paul hurled his thunders against the institution and the temples of idolatry, and laid them in the dust. The first act of the missionary to India is to preach directly or indirectly against the political institutions of the country. Polygamy and divorce were political institutions of the Jews, founded, we are told, on the hardness of the people's hearts; yet Christ denounced them. Is the institution of slavery to find an asylum from the assaults of the pulpit, beneath the wings of the American eagle?

Is not rum-selling a political institution? Is the pulpit therefore to be gagged, and rum's abominations to be permitted to go unchecked? No, in the name of the Lord of Hosts let us cry aloud, spare not, and show to the house of Israel their sins. Let us expose the abomination of slavery in all its hideous deformity; let all arise in the majesty of their might, and, with a more than Carthaginian fidelity, on the altars of our holy Christianity swear eternal hostility to tyranny's rule, and emphatically affirm that the virgin soil of America shall not be prostituted to the spread and perpetuation of the wrongs and outrages of Africa. Amen.